THE DARKNESS OF WATER

MATTHEW NEIGHBOURS

The Darkness of Water / Matthew Neighbours
ISBN: 978-0-9986525-0-4
Cover art by Neighbour Bros. Media LLC

CONTENTS

Chapter 1

JAMES AND ELENA: DAY 1

There was something about the water down below from where James stood. It was dark, menacing, yet somehow inviting. It almost seemed to be calling out to him, how the gentle waves crashed on the rocky shore and swirled around. He had thought about it many times before, but only in jest. He never seriously intended on going through with it—at least that's what he told himself.

The water's edge formed a semicircle at the foot of the cliffs, which went straight down and even receded slightly as they came to where the gentle waves broke upon the face of the rock. Toward either end of this half-circle, a thin bar of land started to appear between the water and the face of the cliff. The water here was quite deep. James had confirmed this the day before by swimming in the area.

There was a darkness in those waters though, a living, breathing darkness—and as James thought now, a beautiful darkness. As he stared into the water, becoming more and more mesmerized by it, it was almost as if there was some kind of living entity beneath the surface. Something that seemed to latch onto his mind, separating him from reality and into a world that consisted of only himself and the water below.

Yes, he could see it now—it was not water at all, but a gateway. A swirling black hole that would take him into another existence. And without even realizing it, he was leaning forward more and more. He was thinking about the dark waves wrapping around him, taking him in, and bringing him below. Taking him away from this world. His mind started to drift—

A scream snapped him out of his trance. Reality flooded back in as James looked up. Out of the corner of his eye, he saw someone fall into the water with a splash. The person had fallen from the same cliff not twenty yards away.

Instinct kicked in and he jumped, falling through the air. Plunging into the dark water, the cold hit him immediately and for a moment he couldn't see anything with the whirlwind of bubbles rising up from all around him. Then, off in the distance, he saw a shadowy shape of what looked like a person. James swam as fast as he could toward the shape. He could now clearly see her—a woman—she wasn't moving, just slowly sinking deeper into the water. James grabbed her in his arms and swam to the surface. After gasping for air, he carried her toward the area where the thin rocky strip of land appeared, the beginning shoreline that separated the cliff from the water.

After struggling to swim while holding onto another body, he made it to the shore and gently laid her down. She still wasn't moving or breathing so far as he could tell. James had never performed CPR before, but he was pretty sure he knew what to do—it seemed simple enough from what he'd seen. He hesitantly placed both hands on her chest. *Okay, breathe, you can do this,* he thought as he started doing chest compressions. *Shit, how many times am I supposed to do this?* He was about to stop after ten, then decided to do five more. Still nothing. He tilted her head up slightly, and while pinching her nose, breathed into her mouth. Once, then twice. *I sure hope I'm doing this right,* he thought again as he started chest compressions a second time.

He was at seventeen compressions when she suddenly came to, coughing up water and gasping for air. She looked up at him with an expression that James couldn't read. But if he had to guess, he thought he saw a mixture of anxiety and fear, and perhaps something else that he couldn't quite place. Whatever it was, it wasn't what he expected to see in someone who had just been resuscitated.

She didn't say anything at first and just stared up at him. He simply stared back at her, feeling amazed that his CPR had actually worked, and now that she was conscious having no idea what he should do next. Before the silence—which already felt very long and strange between them—drew on any further, he finally asked, "Are you okay?"

"Yes, I ... I think so," the woman said after a brief hesitation, still looking up at him. "What happened?"

"You don't remember? You fell from those cliffs up there. I was worried you might have hit a rock on the way down, or that you would drown before I pulled you out. But you seem to be okay now."

"Yes, I think I am, thanks to you," she said as she slowly got to her feet. "I'm lucky that you were here to save me. What are the chances, huh?"

"I was just in the right place at the right time, I guess. It's odd, though—you're the first person I've seen around here. What were you doing up there?"

"I was just taking a walk, and then ... I don't know. I don't remember." She looked away from him as she spoke, then took a seat on a rock. "I guess I must have slipped and fell, I just don't remember."

As he looked into her eyes, he thought that she remembered more than what she was telling him. But why would she lie about that? Unless it really wasn't an accident. Regardless of her intentions, if any, this wasn't the time to question her. But he couldn't seem to shake that thought, and then it brought an even more troubling question to his mind, one that he immediately tried to dismiss—why was *he* up on that cliff?

As James looked over at her again, he saw a sadness in her eyes, but there was something else in those eyes too, something dark and mysterious, something he couldn't place.

"My name is James," he said. "James Torbour."

"I'm Elena."

"Well, Elena, I'm staying at a house that's only a short way from here." James pointed toward where the coastline receded out of view about a mile away. "You're welcome to come rest a little, and let your clothes dry before continuing on to wherever you're going. And I could feel better knowing that you're okay."

"James, I really am okay, and I wouldn't want to put you out or anything. I'm fine, really," Elena said as she took her shoes off, wringing the water out of them with her hands.

"It's no trouble. You would actually be doing me a favor, as I get little company out here." James sat down on a rock not far from hers and took off the light jacket that he was wearing. He twisted it in hands, trying to squeeze every last bit of water out of it. It was made of a light-brown cloth and was as absorbent as a sponge.

Elena slipped back into her shoes and stood up. "In that case, I suppose I wouldn't mind a little rest, thank you."

James hopped up and put his jacket back on. "You ready to get going then? It's not too far."

"Yeah, I think so."

They started walking south along the coast, with the water on their right and the cliffs to their left. They were on a bay of the Pacific Ocean. Across this bay was another shore that had mountains running along most of its length.

As James led the way, he kept looking back at Elena. Partly he just wanted to make sure she hadn't wandered off. She was silent as she followed behind him, and sometimes he couldn't hear her footsteps at all. But there was more to it than just that. She was attractive, with blonde hair that hung several inches past her shoulders in its currently wet state. It looked as if her mind was somewhere else, a very sad and worrisome place. It almost seemed like she was holding on to some dark past or terrible secret, and judging by what had just happened, James didn't doubt that she was. When she caught him looking at her, she smiled back at him—a deliberate, mechanical smile.

When they came around the bend, the narrow band of shoreline expanded to a full-blown beach, first sand and then rocks. Situated a half mile down this sandy shoreline, and set back a little from the rocky barrier separating the sand and the weeds, was a house standing in front of a forest that had replaced the sheer cliffs pressing against the water's edge. It was a fairly big house, with two stories, and looked like it was new and modern, but still with a rustic feel to it. Directly in front of the house, the land jutted farther into the water than the shoreline off to either side of it, making the house feel closer to the water than it otherwise would've been. The forest behind the house quickly rose up to a beautiful mountain backdrop. The panorama before them was like something out of a postcard, and was also very secluded, as there wasn't another house or any sign of people to be seen anywhere.

As they got closer to the house, Elena saw just how nice it was. The structure seemed to evoke a welcoming warmth with its exposed light brown logs and grey slate shingled roof. In the house's front, overlooking the ocean, was a wooden deck surrounded by a short railing with an overhanging roof. Above the first-story roof and behind the porch were two banks of large windows. A short stone stairway led up the rocky strip that separated the sandy beach and the grassy area several feet above it, then to a brick path leading to the house. The house did, in fact, look very new, and actually a little out of place here all by itself in these wild woods and empty shoreline. The yard around the house had been mowed, and there was a fenced-in garden off to the right side.

As they approached the doorway, James noticed that Elena was shivering in the wind coming off the ocean. It struck him that all she had on was a thin long-sleeve shirt, once a faded orange and now dark with water. James felt stupid that he hadn't offered her his jacket. He ran up the path and opened the door, then beckoned her inside.

"I'm sorry, I didn't realize how cold it had gotten. I'll get a fire going."

As Elena entered the house, she walked past the small hallway and gazed at the interior of the room that opened in front of her. Running her hand along the wall that continued straight ahead on her right, she walked forward until it opened up into the kitchen. She gave the space a lingering glance, noticing the marble countertops, and how modern all the appliances were. A dining table stood in front of large sliding glass doors, looking out at the ocean.

Elena walked back into the main large room of the house. Her eyes gravitated to the large stone fireplace against the back wall. Immense windows on the other two walls bathed the room in sunlight. The thought struck her that none of this seemed to fit James at all. Of course, that was ridiculous, seeing as how she had just met him. She leaned against one of the three couches that sat around a glass coffee table in the middle of the room. Something felt off about it all, though.

James came in carrying a box of firewood and went over to the fireplace. Elena looked around the room again, at the gleaming hardwood flooring and the whole size and décor of the place in general. It didn't look like the home of a man living alone, if he actually was living alone—she hadn't asked.

James now had a fire going in the fireplace, burning large and bright. "Come and sit by the fire," he said. "It'll warm you up and dry your clothes."

"This house is beautiful," Elena said as she walked over to the fire, still looking around at the living room. "Is it yours, or are you just house sitting or something?"

"Umm, yeah, it ... it belongs to a friend of mine, actually. I'm just staying here for a bit. I needed to get away for a little while, you know. Have some time to sort things out, away from everything."

Elena stared intently at him, as if trying to discern whether he was telling her the truth. "I know the feeling," she finally said. "So you're here alone, then? The quiet can get to you if you're not careful, especially out here."

"It sounds like you're speaking from experience. Do live around here then?"

"Well, loneliness can start to eat at you anywhere, but it seems to be more than that out here. It's beautiful, but there's a darkness as well. I'm just saying that you might not want to spend too much time around here, especially if you're alone."

There was a moment of silence before James spoke again. "Yes, perhaps. But it was the quiet that drew me to this place to begin with. When I found—was asked if I wanted to take care of the house for a little while, that was one of the things I loved about it. I guess I've always enjoyed solitude to some extent, sometimes it can be better company than people. I've always had a hard time relating to most people, though."

James turned his head from the fire to look Elena in the eyes. "Maybe I've just been waiting for—" He broke off and looked back into the fire. Then he said with a change of tone, "I hope the fire is warm enough ... I can always go and get more wood."

"No, it's fine." Elena wanted to believe James, to trust him. There was something about him that made her want to ignore the warning signs in her head. For some reason she couldn't explain, she desperately wanted to believe that he was different, different from the others she had come across. But there was one thing he'd said that really stuck out in her head, that he'd *found* this house before correcting himself. Why would he say that? It could be nothing, or he could have slipped up in a lie.

There was something wrong here, and Elena was determined to find out what it was. But as she was resolving to, she suddenly realized how tired she was. And as she was staring into the bright flames of the fire, her eyes grew very heavy and she slowly laid down right there on the floor.

Chapter 2

JAMES AND ELENA: DAY 1, PART 2

Elena found herself walking through the woods. It was night and everything was very dark. She didn't know where she was going, but somehow it felt like her feet knew exactly where to go. The darkness seemed to close in around her, the trees leaning in as she walked, the path getting narrower and narrower. The constant chirping of crickets, the hoot of an owl, the howl of a wolf, all grew louder, converging into an unbearable dissonance of noise. An owl swooped down right above her head, making her fall down onto the ground. The fear inside her started to grow as she got back to her feet. As she continued to walk forward, she wanted to scream but felt unable to. She was just about to break into a run when the woods opened into a clearing, and out in front of her there was a house.

The house seemed familiar to her, but she couldn't seem to place it exactly. She felt some relief from being out of the woods, but found little comfort in the sight of that house. Some strange kind of fog surrounded it, and a darkness darker than the night itself seemed to emanate from within it. Something that you could almost feel, like you could reach out and touch it with your hand. She didn't want to enter the house, in fact she was deathly afraid to. In that moment, she would have rather turned around and ran back into the dark woods that had just harried her, but she couldn't stop herself from walking forward.

Suddenly, Elena was walking down a corridor with evenly spaced doors on either side. The sense of familiarity came back; somehow she knew she had been here before but still couldn't place it. The fear was steadily building with each step that she took. Her vision started to spin, her legs turned to rubber, but still she kept moving forward. Then at the end of the corridor there was a door, no different in color or appearance and yet somehow not the same as the others. "No ... no, I can't go in there. Not through the door ... not through *that* door," she was saying to herself. She suddenly had flashes of being somewhere else—there was a bed. She was on the bed, could feel the silk sheets beneath her, and she heard certain sounds. Sounds of pleasure? Sounds of pain? She couldn't tell. Was she the one making these sounds? Elena just wanted to get out of there, but she couldn't stop herself from continuing to walk forward. She found herself in front of the door and was already turning the doorknob. The door opened and a man stood in front of her. *No, not him.* And then, just like that she knew where she was. She knew exactly what this place was and how she had been here before. *It can't be him. I can't be here.* Having no control over her body, she walked right into his embrace and kissed him—

"NO!" Elena shouted, sitting straight up, her heart racing. It took a moment for her mind to catch up to what her eyes were seeing, and then she realized that she was still in the living room of James's house. The fire had burned down to a faint flicker of what it had been before. She looked outside—it was still light out, though the sun was getting ready to set.

She found the bathroom, just down a hall from the living room, then went to the kitchen. She took a glass from one of the cabinets and filled it at the sink. As she drank the water, she wondered how this house was able to have all the modern conveniences out in the middle of nowhere. Then she wondered where James was—maybe he was upstairs or outside. The thought struck her that she should look around the house. This was the perfect opportunity to see whether there really was something wrong here. She had a feeling that he wasn't friends with, or even knew the owner as he claimed. Normally, she wouldn't be so nosy, but she knew that something wasn't right. James was lying about something, and she had to know what it was.

Elena started going through the kitchen drawers. She didn't know what she was looking for, maybe a name, like on a piece of mail, maybe something more, just something to tell her whether she was right about him or whether she was simply being paranoid.

She found nothing in the kitchen, so she moved to the living room. After going through several more drawers, tables, and cabinets along the walls, she still hadn't found anything of interest. She made her way down the hallway leading toward the back of the house. The hall was fairly open, with a vaulted ceiling and a stairway on her left that cut back toward the front of the house.

At the top of the stairs was another hallway with a small window on either end. Elena turned right and then found an open door to her left. As she entered the room, she saw that it was a spacious bedroom with a king-sized bed. There was a large window looking outside, not quite as big as the picture windows downstairs, but still quite large. With the sun coloring the ocean red, orange, and purple, it really was quite a spectacular view, and Elena found herself just staring out the window for several minutes. When she finally pulled her gaze away, she saw a doorway leading into a bathroom—this had to be the master bedroom.

There were closets on either side of the bed. Elena went over and opened the closet on the left side of the bed and found it full of clothes on hangers, all of them men's clothes. The other closet was full of women's clothes. *A husband and wife probably, that makes sense considering the size of the house. But that still doesn't mean anything. I have to keep looking for something more.*

Elena walked over to the other side of the hall and found another bedroom, this one smaller, but still with a large window looking out. There was no attached bathroom and only one closet. The closet was mostly empty, with only two shirts hanging up in it, and the bed was unmade. On the floor at the foot of the bed was a partially open roller bag with a few clothes spilling out from it. Elena unzipped the bag fully and found that it was still almost full with clothes. It seemed that this must be the room James was staying in, and that he hadn't fully moved in. Maybe he had just arrived? *There has to be something, something here that can at least point to who the real owners of this house are. That might be enough to at least know for sure whether James is lying.*

She went back to the master bedroom. She searched through the drawers of the bedside table, and through the pockets of shirts and pants in both closets. Still nothing. *Where are all the photos? Doesn't every house have family photos?* She hadn't seen any, which she thought was rather odd.

The bathroom, she hadn't looked through there yet. A moment later, Elena was rummaging through the cabinets. Makeup, cosmetics, shaving cream, razors, Advil, various other items, but no prescriptions, nothing with a name on it. *Why is there nothing to point me to a name? Why is this so difficult?* She looked down at the garbage can, which was almost full. Hesitantly she reached down and rummaged through the garbage, empty cardboard boxes of toothpaste and toilet paper rolls, tissues—*is that hair, this is so gross*—"Yes!" Elena blurted out. A prescription bottle. *Truosetine ... Green, Anna. Finally, a name. No idea what Truosetine is, but that doesn't matter, I have a name. It still doesn't prove anything for sure, but it's something—*

"Elena, are you up here?"

Shit. Elena could hear James climbing the stairs. She dropped the bottle back into the can, then hastily covered it with tissues and other garbage. She wiped her hands on her pants, not having time to wash them off, and made it back into the bedroom just as James walked in.

"There you are, I was worried you might have left." James looked at her with a warm smile. "How did you sleep?"

"Fine, I guess. I didn't realize how tired I was. When I didn't see you around, I decided to take a look at the rest of the house. Where were you?"

"I was in the garden. I didn't want to wake you, and figured you probably needed the sleep, you know, with the day that you've had."

"You mean with me almost drowning? Yes, I guess it took more out of me than I thought." She wanted to confront him right there and then. To hear him tell her a perfectly reasonable explanation for why he had lied to her. She found herself wanting to trust him again. But she needed more information. One name wasn't enough to tell how far this lie went. So she said nothing more.

They went back downstairs and Elena gazed out the big picture window again. The sun had now set behind the darkening horizon. Lost in thought, she jumped slightly when she felt a hand touch her shoulder.

"I'm sorry," James said. "I didn't mean to ... well, the tea's ready. Is there something wrong? I just wish ..." He stood there for a moment, not knowing how to finish his sentence, glancing out the window at the dark clouds that were beginning to move in. "Seems like a storm is coming." He looked over at her. "Elena, I can drive you back home, or to your car, or wherever you want. We might even make it before the rain if we leave now, if that's what you want. But you're more than welcome to stay the night."

Elena knew she should say no, that she couldn't trust him, that she might even be in danger staying here. But she also felt she needed to get to the bottom of whatever was going on. And as much as she wanted to, she couldn't forget why she was here, regardless of whether he was lying or not. Looking out the window, she whispered, almost as if to herself, "It's so dark out there." Then she turned and looked at James. "Well, maybe just for the night. That is, if you're sure I wouldn't be a bother."

"Not at all. I'll get some food together. If you want, you can go ahead and take a shower. There's one attached to the room I found you in upstairs. I've been sleeping in a different room, so that one is all yours."

"A shower would be great, thank you," Elena said. She really did need a shower, feeling the dried salt caked on her skin, and the griminess of it in her hair.

She went upstairs and undressed. The hot shower felt so good, it was hard to tear herself away. But Elena knew she had to hurry up and look over the room once more for any more clues that she might have missed.

When she walked out of the shower, she went over to her clothes lying on the floor. She picked them up, then let them fall. They felt so grimy in her hands. She walked over to the woman's closet, Anna Green's. Elena didn't want to wear some stranger's clothes, but seeing that they were in her size, she overcame the awkwardness that she was feeling. She picked out a white sweater and black fleece pants, and after some hesitation, dressed in the woman's underwear from the dresser as well.

Then she quickly started to go through the room again, trying to think of any places where she hadn't looked the first time. She searched more thoroughly through drawers that she had previously only breezed through. Then she bent down and looked under the bed—the wooden floor was completely bare. Wait, there was something wedged behind one of the bedposts, a picture frame. She crawled back out with it and sat down on the bed. There was a spidery crack in the glass, and beneath that, a photograph. A man and a woman with the ocean behind them at sunset. They were smiling and looked genuinely happy, but the photo itself wasn't what struck Elena. It was the words that were written over it.

She Is Dead

The words were scrawled over the woman in the photograph in bold black marker.

"Shit," Elena said to herself. "What the hell is going on here?" She pulled the photograph out of the frame and turned it over. *Mr. George Green and Mrs. Anna Green, Maui, 2008* was written in calligraphy.

If James is at the heart of whatever is going on here, it's worse than I thought. But then again, if it is James at the heart of whatever this is, it will make what I have to do all the easier. No, stop it, it doesn't make anything easier. It could be him. *You know that more than likely it's* him, *not James, who's behind all this. Whatever all this is. I have to confront James. But I have to be careful about how I do it.*

Elena folded the photo in half and stuck it in her pocket, then made her way downstairs, where she saw

James fussing with the oven. She just stood there and watched him until he turned around with a baking sheet in his hand.

James froze. He looked like he was about to say something, but then thought better of it.

"I'm sorry, I hope you don't mind," Elena said. "I found these in the closet and I thought it would be all right if I wore them. I can go right back up and change though if you—"

"No. No it's fine. You look beautiful. My friend—his wife, I mean, I'm sure she wouldn't mind."

"Her name?"

"What?"

"What's her name? The woman of whose clothes I'm wearing."

"Oh, right. It's Katherine."

Elena knew he was lying to her now, and she was almost as sure that it showed on her face. The only thing left was to find out why and how deep this lie went.

After a moment of silence passed between them, James finally said, "Well, the food's getting cold. How about we sit down and eat?"

"Yes, it smells delicious," Elena said, inhaling the scent of garlic bread filling the room.

"I hope you like pasta. I probably should've asked beforehand."

"I love it," she replied. Although realizing that she had eaten nothing since that morning, and then almost drowned, she would've been happy to eat anything.

Neither James nor Elena said much while they ate. It was rather an awkward silence. Elena was trying to figure out what she needed to say, and James simply didn't know what he could say.

After they finished eating, James knew he had to say something. "Elena, I can tell that there's something bothering you. When I look at you, it seems ... like you're somewhere else. If there's anything you want to talk about, I know you don't know me, but if you need to talk to anyone, I'm here. You can trust me; I would love to help you if I can."

"Trust you? That isn't the first time that someone's given me that line. You have no idea who I even am, and I surely don't know you." Suddenly all the caution and delicacy that Elena planned to approach this matter with went right out the window. "Why would I ever fucking trust you!"

"What?" James asked, startled by this sudden outburst of anger. "What are you talking about? What's the matter?"

"Katherine, who the hell is she? Because I'm betting she has nothing to do with this house!"

"What do you mean? Elena, calm down and we—"

"Calm down! No, you know damn well what I'm talking about. How did you really come upon this house? What did you do to them?"

"What? I didn't do anything."

Elena pulled the photograph out of her pocket and threw it on the table. "George and Anna. Now do you know what I'm talking about?"

James looked at the photo for several moments with a puzzled expression on his face. "Whatever you think is going on, whatever you think I apparently did, you're mistaken. I've never seen this before, I don't even know—"

Elena got up from her chair, which made a loud grating noise across the hardwood as it slid back, and almost ran from the table, going over to the big window in the living room.

Oh shit, James thought, starting to have some realization of what she was accusing him of. He stood up from his chair and walked over to Elena. It was now dark outside, and the window reflected her troubled face. "Elena..."

"You know," Elena said, still looking out the window, "when I first met you, when I first looked into your eyes after you brought me back to consciousness ... I thought you might be different. I thought I saw a quality that set you apart from the other people that I've known. That's a stupid way to feel about someone only from an initial look at them, I know. I guess it's probably just because you saved me that I felt that way. I thought you were ..."

Tears started to slide down Elena's face. "With everything that's happened to me, with everything I've been going through, I thought that you might have been the one good thing to happen to me. I guess I was wrong."

"Elena, I'm sorry. I'm sorry I lied to you. But it's not what you think. I should have been completely honest from the start. I guess I thought it would be easier—to tell you the whole truth right away just seemed too difficult. It's not something I can just sum up in a sentence or two. It's true that I don't know the owners of this house, but I didn't come here by any nefarious means. I never did anything to this George and Anna. I'll tell you the complete story now, though, if you're willing to listen."

He paused, and when Elena stayed silent, he continued. "About a month ago, I decided I couldn't keep living the same life I had been living. I was sick of the meaningless job that I'd had for years, working without any real purpose or future, just a paycheck to get me through the weeks. And my personal life wasn't much better—I've never been able to fit in with the rest of the world. After a while I just couldn't take it any more, and just had to get away and try to find something else, something real. I was living in a crappy apartment in Rockford, Illinois, west of Chicago, and for a while I'd had this idea of moving to Alaska. I'm not sure why I always had Alaska in mind, perhaps because of the beauty of the mountains and ocean. You don't see a lot of that where I'm from.

"I saved up some money and quit my job. I went to Washington first, then drove up through Canada. Beyond getting to Alaska, though, I didn't have a plan. I drifted around a while just looking for something, but I don't think I ever fully understood what that something was. What I was looking for wasn't really a specific place, but more like a feeling. It's like an idea of a place in your head, but it's abstract, and I guess to boil it down it's not much more than to find a state of purpose and belonging. You probably don't know what I mean. It's hard to put into words."

"I do know what you mean, more than you know." Elena looked at James with a new softness and understanding in her face.

James restarted the fire, and they sat on the couch watching the flames.

"Anyway, I never found what I was looking for," James continued. "After a while, I found myself driving on some gravel road through the mountains in the middle of nowhere. I wasn't completely sure where I was, or even how I got there. Just as I was about to turn around, I saw this grassy dirt road barely wide enough for a car. I stopped my car and just looked down it for a while. I wasn't sure if it was a road, a driveway, or just some, you know, forest service thing. But I had this feeling, like something was compelling me to go down it. So I turned my car and started driving. It felt like almost a mile before I finally got to the end. There was a little clearing in the woods and a small garage. No one appeared to be there."

James looked over at Elena and saw that she was patiently listening to his story. He had been talking rather slowly, deliberately taking his time. Now he picked up his pace as he continued. "As I got out, I could kind of make out a house behind the trees. There was a footpath alongside the garage, and then the trees opened back up and I could see it. A beautiful house by the ocean. *This* house. It struck me as one of the most beautiful and perfect places to live.

"It was getting late, so I decided to ask if I could stay the night. When I knocked, no one answered. I was about to leave, but something inside me said that I should try opening the door. So I turned the doorknob and it was unlocked. I thought that was strange, especially when it turned out that no one was home. I figured it would be okay if I stayed for just one night, thinking that it might be a vacation home or something. But after that night, I didn't want to leave, and didn't have anywhere else to go. There was something else though, a feeling like this was where I belonged. I know this sounds strange to say, but I felt like I had some purpose to fulfill here. I kept going back and forth on it, but then I decided I would stay here for a bit, keep the house in the same condition and if the owners came back while I was still here I would explain the situation and give them some money. That was ten days ago now."

James looked into the fire, rubbing his hand across the stubble on his chin. "I don't know, but when I was outside while you were sleeping, I thought that maybe the reason for staying here was to save your life, that maybe God brought me to this house, and maybe he put me up on that ridge at that very moment to save your life. Maybe that was my purpose, what brought me all this way from Illinois. I don't know what happened to the owners of this house, to George and Anna, if anything even did happen to them. They might just be in California somewhere. This doesn't really seem like a permanent residence out in the middle of nowhere like this. Anyway, I never saw them. I know you don't have any reason to believe me, but this is the truth."

They sat there in silence, and then while looking at the fire, Elena quietly said, "I believe you."

"Thank you, Elena, that means a lot."

Elena still wasn't sure that she really did, in fact, believe him, but she wanted to. She just needed some time to process everything before she could know what to think. "Look, even with my nap earlier, I'm still tired. Do mind if I call it a night?"

"No, of course. It's been a ... a long day. Here, I'll show you to your room."

"No, that's okay. I know where it is."

James blushed. "Of course you do. Well, I'll be right down the hall if you need anything."

Elena went upstairs and fell onto the bed, her head swimming with thoughts. Could she trust him? She thought about the way he talked when he told her his story, the earnestness in his voice. The way he looked at her when he asked her to believe him. The subtle wave in his short brown hair, the stubble on his firm chin. *No! I can't feel this way about him. I have to remember why I'm here. You better hope that he was lying. If he really is who he says he is, that makes everything so much harder. What am I going to do if he really is a good person?*

Chapter 3

GEORGE AND ANNA: SEVEN MONTHS EARLIER

"To our new house," George said, lifting a glass of red wine.

"To new beginnings," Anna replied, lifting her own glass. She took a good drink and then took a bite of her steak. "I know it's later then it was supposed to be, but we're here now, we did it."

"'Unforeseen complications,'" George muttered. "How many times did we hear those words in the last three months?"

After almost two years of planning, George and Anna Green had finally made their move from Anchorage into their newly constructed home one hundred and forty miles to the south, on a mostly isolated coastline on the Kenai Peninsula, east of Resurrection Bay and the city of Seward.

"I know you wanted to enjoy the summer while we settled in here," Anna said, "but we still have the fall. September's not the same as June, but it'll be great, you'll see."

"Having you here and seeing you so happy is all I need."

"Oh, is that right? So this big house, this beautiful view we can look at even while we're sitting here eating? That's all what, nothing?"

"That's just icing on the cake, and none of it would matter if you weren't here with me."

Anna was looking out the window, out across the bay and to the stretch of mountains that separated them from Seward. The sun had already set, but some of its light still lingered on the horizon. "No, this isn't just icing, it's beautiful." Anna turned to face George and smiled. "It's perfect."

"Well, perfect is what I was kind of going for," George said as he smiled back.

"Will it always be this isolated here, do you think? Or are we going to have neighbors around here soon?"

"Hard to say. Ten, twenty years, and maybe. But until they run power lines out here, it's only going to be a few isolated homes with people that wanted to get away from civilization and live off the grid, people like you and me."

"I hope it stays just the way it is. But I do worry that it will be too much for you after a while. We're so far away from all our friends back in Anchorage."

"They'll still visit now and again, and we can still visit them. Jack was down here just a week ago. And Seward is only a half-hour drive away."

Anna wrinkled her nose. "I guess there wasn't much left to miss. I already drove most of our friends away while we were still in the city."

"That wasn't your fault, and it doesn't matter anyway," George said. "I'll be fine out here. Between hunting and fishing, and writing that book that I can finally dedicate some time to, I'll have more than enough to keep myself busy. And most of all I have you, and as long as you're happy, I'm happy. We have a new start, a new life."

"I am happy, and there's so much inspiration out here for my art that I should be able to keep busy myself. I can't believe this is really happening, that we really did it. It's been so long since I've believed in a real future for us, for me."

Anna looked deeply into his eyes, trying to convey all the feeling and meaning that she meant to show in her next two words. With true heartfelt emotion that only George could fully understand, she said, "Thank you."

After they finished eating, George looked across the table over at Anna. "So, how about we go upstairs and officially break this house in?"

"I seem to remember already doing that—or did you forget?"

"Well, that was before we were actually moved in, so it doesn't count." George got up and held out his hand. Anna took it, and he led her past cardboard boxes strewn across the floor, some of them partially unpacked and some still waiting to be opened. Then they made their way up the stairs.

Chapter 4

JAMES AND ELENA: DAY 2

James woke up to see light shining through his window. While heading toward the stairs, he glanced over at the door to Elena's room. It was slightly ajar, and he briefly wondered if she was still inside. He resisted an urge to look inside and turned and went down the stairs. As he rounded the corner into the kitchen, he saw her standing in front of the window by the dining table, drinking from a mug that she held in both hands. She wore a white and grey flannel shirt with the sleeves rolled up, and she had her hair up in a loose bun that still let some of it fall down. It struck him again how beautiful she was, but he tried to put that thought away, trying not to think about things that he knew would never happen.

"Good morning," he said. "I can make some breakfast, what would you like?"

"I'm not hungry, but go ahead and make something for yourself," Elena said, still looking out the window. The sky was just getting light from the rising sun.

"Okay," James said cautiously. "You're more than welcome to stay here as long as you like, you know. It's just that ... if there's anything I can do ... you know, to help ... with anything, all you have to do is ask."

After a moment, Elena turned to face James, and the look on her face troubled him. She looked sad, but more than that there was fear. "I ... I don't know what I'm doing here," she said in a voice so quiet that James could barely hear her.

"Elena?" James asked hesitantly. Her face had taken on a vacant look as she stared ahead, not at James, but at some indeterminate point beyond him. He slowly walked up to her and said her name one more time as he reached out and touched her shoulder.

She instinctively jerked away from his touch, and a fierceness hardened her eyes. Then the sudden look of anger left her face almost as quickly as it had come, replaced by a look of sadness.

They stood like that for a little while, then James finally spoke again. "I understand that I don't know what's going on with you, what you're going through. Whatever it is, you don't have to go through it alone. Maybe I can help you somehow, and perhaps that's why we came into each other's lives."

Elena heard the words as if they came from some other place, echoing back in her head over and over again. *Maybe I can help you somehow, help you somehow, help you—* "Help me?" Her eyes flashed once more. "No James, you can't help me, it's much too late for that. You have no idea what is really going on, what's really out there. What's the worst situation you've ever been in? Maybe if you can get off your high horse and stop thinking that you can fix everyone's problems without having the slightest clue of what they're going through, then maybe you can stop coming off as a self-righteous prick and maybe, just maybe, actually end up helping instead of making matters worse."

"Elena, I'm sorry, I didn't mean to—"

"No, of course you didn't mean to. People like you never *mean to*, do they?" Elena brushed past him and yanked open the front door.

"Wait, where are you going?"

"I just need some fresh air. I—" She stopped and looked back at him, still holding the open door. "I'm sorry." She let the door close behind her and started walking down the path toward the water's edge. Thoughts were running through her head in a chaotic mess. She forced herself to stop and think. Glancing back, she saw James looking at her through the big window. She was glad to see that he had resisted following her, probably sensing it was best to leave her be for now. *I have to leave; I have to get away. What am I doing here? I shouldn't have said that to him, but he can't help, and he has to realize that.* Elena thought about the feeling that she'd had when she got up that morning. The feeling that she really did believe James, that he wasn't like the other men she'd known before. There was something different about him. *No, I can't leave. I came here for a reason, and I have to stay. I have to figure out a way to deal with this, running away won't solve anything.*

And with that final thought, Elena turned and walked back into the house. "I didn't mean to go off on you like that," she said, calm now. "Sometimes I let my emotions get the best of me. I'm sorry. And for last night, too. I had jumped to conclusions, and the way I reacted wasn't fair. Look ... there are things I can't talk about right now. But if your offer still stands, I would like to stay here a little longer, if that's still okay."

"Of course you can still stay, and I'm sorry too. Your life is your own, and it's none of my business if you don't want it to be."

Elena smiled. "All right, enough of all that. I think I might actually be hungry now, so how 'bout we go ahead with that breakfast after all."

"I was thinking," Elena said as she finished eating the last of the scrambled eggs on her plate. "Where are George and Anna? I mean, their clothes are all still here, and I'm starting to doubt that this was a vacation home. And then that picture I found, I just get this feeling that something terrible has happened to them."

"Yes, it does seem strange, but I don't think we should rush to conclusions," James said. "That picture aside, which might not mean anything, there are many reasons why they could be gone."

"I suppose so, but something doesn't seem right. I just can't place my finger on it. The electricity is still working, there's still running water, and you had said the door was unlocked when you arrived. But if something really did happen to them, wouldn't there be people out looking for them? Wouldn't this place be boarded up, or for sale? Unless it just recently happened and no one has realized it yet. They are kind of out in the middle of nowhere, so it might take some time before people noticed they were missing."

"As far as electricity goes, I was out walking one day and saw some kind of machinery down by the small river not far from here. There was a turbine that a small waterfall was falling into, which I think is producing the electricity here, and it seems to be very self-sustaining. I'm pretty sure they also have some kind of well for water. Even being so close to the ocean, I heard that there would still be freshwater that floats on top of the saltwater, that you would be able to collect with a certain kind of well. So everything just runs on its own, whether anyone's here or not."

"Yeah, I guess," Elena said. "But I still think something could have happened and nobody knows. I don't get any kind of reception out here. Do they have a landline?"

"Not that I've seen. But maybe they have some kind of satellite phone."

"The trees are really something out here," Elena said as she gazed up at the Sitka spruce towering above her.

James looked over at her but didn't say anything. He kept fiddling with the handgun strapped to his belt, hoping that it had the stopping power to put down a bear, in the unlikely possibility that he would ever have to use it. They were almost a mile into the forest now, not walking on any trail, but there wasn't much undergrowth and there was plenty of space to walk between the trees. They were at the foot of the mountain now and came up to a steep incline. James found a way up that didn't look too difficult, but still required climbing up some rocks.

"Just follow the footholds that I use and you shouldn't have too much trouble getting up," James said as he started to make his way up. Carefully looking for the path of least resistance, and after slipping a little only once, he reached the top.

When Elena reached the top, she slipped and fell partially into James's arms as he caught her. After glancing up at his face, she stepped away from him. Then, after a brief rest, they continued to walk on.

"James," Elena said, breaking the silence that was in the air, "maybe I shouldn't say anything, but ... is there something going on here? I mean ... never mind, I shouldn't have said anything. Forget it."

"What do you mean?" James asked.

"It's just that ... if you're expecting more from this, from me, don't. You seem like a nice guy and all, and I appreciate everything you've done for me, but things can't go any further than this. I just figured I should be up front about it."

"Look, as far as I'm concerned we're just two people out on a walk, enjoying each other's company. There doesn't have to be anything more to it than that." But as he tried to reassure her, he felt a mixture of relief and sadness at what she had said.

"It's just that I've been through some stuff recently, and I'm not ready to start any kind of ... anything, with someone right now."

"Elena, there's no need to explain, I get it. I'm fine with ... I'm happy to have you here for as long as you want to be. Let's just leave it at that. You don't need to worry."

"Right, good." Elena was suddenly very embarrassed. She felt like an idiot and wished she could just take back everything she had just said. She didn't even know herself why she felt the need to tell him all that. Perhaps it was because she feared he might try to make a move on her. Or maybe there was a part of her that felt something more for him, and she was trying to convince herself otherwise. Whatever the reason, she had chosen to stay here for another reason, and she couldn't let something like that interfere.

After that, neither of them said much as they continued to walk through the woods.

It was early afternoon now; they had eaten a lunch of ham and cheese sandwiches and fruit after they had come back to the house. They were now sitting on the deck, looking out over the water.

"Know how to fish?" James asked.

"Yeah," Elena replied, still gazing at the ocean.

"How about we catch some dinner then? I'm tired of eating out of the freezer. Come on, maybe you can give me some pointers."

They went into the small shed next to the garden and gathered up two fishing poles and a tackle box. Then they walked south along the shore until they came to the small river that poured out into the ocean. They hiked a little ways upstream before stopping along its edge.

"I've caught some trout in here before," James said. "I think it's too early in the year for any salmon, though."

They quickly caught a few small fish, and then after a while nothing was biting.

"Maybe I shouldn't say anything. I do like having you here," James said as they sat near the edge of the river, "but

... isn't there anywhere you should be getting back to? Family, a place you call home?"

Elena looked away.

"Never mind, I shouldn't have said anything." James thought back to how he had met her yesterday and realized that he probably shouldn't have pushed the matter. "I'm sorry, I didn't mean to pry."

"I just can't talk about it right now." Elena looked up from the water at James. "But no, I have nowhere else I want to go back to right now."

A moment of silence followed between them, and as James looked back at Elena, he had a feeling that he couldn't describe.

"If you don't mind me asking, what did you do here before you met me?" Elena asked. "I mean, it just seems like a very lonely place to be all by yourself."

James leaned back with his hands propped against the ground behind him and gazed up at the sky. "Well, I haven't been here all that long. Only ten days or so, it's not like I had enough time to get bored out of my mind or anything. But okay, let's see. I drove into Seward to stock up on some food and some other supplies. I did that twice, actually. There was quite a bit of hiking I did, up and down the coastline as well as parts of the forest. I fished some, and also read a lot. Otherwise, I pretty much just chilled out and relaxed. You're right though, it did get lonely."

Then James thought about how dark and sad his thoughts had become those last few days, and how often he would end up standing at the edge of that cliff. It was a beautiful view, which was what brought him there at first. But he knew that wasn't the only reason, as he remembered how he would stare down at the water far below him. He thought about what he might have done if Elena hadn't fallen into the water.

"Hey, are you alright?" Elena asked. "It seemed like you were somewhere else there for a minute."

"Hmm, yes," James said as he snapped back to reality. "I'm fine." He stared into the water again for a moment. "Well, the fish aren't biting any more and it's starting to get late. We have enough here for maybe two meals though, so why not head back and fry them up?"

The clouds came back in, along with a thin layer of fog stretching out along the water. James and Elena cleaned the few fish they caught, and then James fried them up on the stove as the rain began to fall outside.

Dinner was similar to the night before, yet different. There was still some awkwardness and tension in the silence between them, but even so, it was more comfortable than what it had been before. There was a feeling in the room, and even though neither of them had quite adjusted to the new dynamic of living together, they were fine with just being in the moment, not feeling any necessity for words.

Even as the rain continued, some light from the setting sun managed to escape through the clouds. James came out of the kitchen after cleaning up and he saw Elena standing on the porch with her back turned toward him. The breeze had picked up and her long blonde hair was blowing gently in the wind. He walked up to her and stood by her side, but slightly behind her. Her blowing hair concealed most of her face, but he could still see that the sadness had come back once again.

"I haven't been entirely truthful with you," Elena said, still staring out into the ocean. "I'm sorry, but sometimes the truth is too hard." Her voice broke a little. "There are things that have happened in my life, things that I've done that I'm not proud of. I can't get into it all right now, but I felt that I had no control over what was happening."

James didn't say anything, and after a long pause, she went on. "I didn't slip and fall into the water ... I jumped. I'm not proud of it now, but I thought it was my only way out of the mess that I'd found myself in. But then, somehow, you were there to save me. I couldn't tell you the truth. I was afraid of what you would think of me. So I lied and told you it was all an accident. Then, after spending some time with you, I started thinking that maybe things could be different, and I know now that death was not the right answer, that maybe there is another way out. I'm sorry, but please don't think poorly of me for what I tried to do, and for lying to you." When she finally turned around to look at him, tears were rolling down her cheeks.

James looked back into her eyes. "No, I don't think poorly of you. You found yourself in a very dark place. Now, I don't know what that was, that's not my business, but I can see that you regret what you did, that you wish you could take it back. Through providence, God's will, fate, whatever you want to call it, I was there to save you. But I think you might have saved me as much as I might have saved you. I'm no stranger to darkness either, the darkness of the mind. The kind that wraps itself around your thoughts and tries to make a home there. It uses the sadness, self-pity, and all the other things that keep your mind headed on a downward path. You have nothing to be sorry for, because when I look at you, I see so much more than the darkness that made you jump, and you have helped me see past that darkness in my own life as well. You made a mistake, but without that mistake I may never have met you, and I am very glad to have met you."

Elena smiled slightly, tears still in her eyes. The sun broke through the clouds a little as it was setting, shining through the gentle rain and shimmering on the rocks ahead of them. James brushed the hair out of Elena's face. Then Elena put her hands around him and hugged him, and James pulled her tightly against himself.

As James held her in his arms, Elena rested her head on his shoulder as a tear fell down her cheek. They stood like that for what seemed like a long time, in that comfortable embrace. Then Elena turned in his arms to look at the sunset, and together they stared out into the horizon, into the unknown. After a while James sensed that Elena was getting tired, so they headed back into the house, holding each other's hands.

They walked up the stairs toward Elena's room still hand in hand. As they stood in front of her door, Elena reluctantly let go of his hand. She leaned against the open door frame and looked at him.

"Goodnight," James said, but he didn't move.

"Goodnight, James." Then, after a moment's more hesitation, she stepped back and slowly closed the door. Pressing her forehead against the wood of the closed door, she let out a sigh. She didn't know exactly how she felt about James, but there was something, the way she felt being held in his arms, the way she hesitated before closing the door. There was a feeling that she felt toward him that was somehow different from the way she had felt toward any other man before. But she had just met him, and what was she really feeling? She collapsed onto the bed and buried her head in the pillow.

"I don't know, I'm so confused," she said to herself as she now stared at the bare wall. "I hate it. It doesn't matter what I'm feeling, none of it does." *I can't let myself develop feelings for this man. I can't let myself feel anything.*

Chapter 5

GEORGE AND ANNA: SIX MONTHS EARLIER

Anna zipped up her jacket as she walked along the shore, feeling the chilly autumn breeze blow in from across the bay. It was the tail end of October, and all the leaves had fallen from the aspens and cottonwoods above her. As she approached the river, she decided to follow it up into the woods, knowing that George was probably still up there looking at the turbine. She listened to the crackle of leaves underneath her feet and the sound of the rushing water—and then George's voice. He was talking to someone. Had one of their friends made an unexpected visit without telling them? She hurried toward the voices. She stopped abruptly when she saw that George was talking to a man she had never seen before, and a wave of fear came over her.

"Anna, come over here," George said. "This is Cole Bontone. And Cole, this is my wife, Anna."

"Pleased to meet you," Cole said as he shook her hand. "I live up on that hill, three or four miles away. I had noticed this house when it was being built and figured I should finally come on down and introduce myself. It's a beautiful place you've set up for yourselves."

"Cole was just helping me fine-tune this turbine. In fact, I think it's running better now than when it was first put in."

"I looked into putting one in at my own place," Cole said, "but I didn't have a good enough source of water nearby. You're lucky with the strong current you get from the glacier."

"It was nice meeting you," Anna said. "I have to get back to the house, though, as I was actually right in the middle of something." She turned and hurried away. When she came back to the shore, she sat on a rock and looked out over the water. Soon, a tear started to roll down her cheek.

"What happened to you?" George asked as he came up behind her a short time later. "That was kind of rude. You know how rare it is to get visitors up here, and now when we find someone who is probably the closest thing we have to a neighbor, you can't wait to rush off."

Anna wiped her face before turning around to face him. "I'm sorry, George. I know how nice it must be for you to meet someone who lives nearby, but—"

"He seems like a straight-up guy. If you just took the time to talk to him, I'm sure you'll agree."

"I know you need to have that interaction with other people than just myself," Anna continued. "I realize it must have been hard for you to leave the city." She paused and looked George sternly in the face. "But I had a feeling. When I saw Cole, a feeling struck me. Like before."

A moment passed between them. "No, you're not going to do this again," George said. "We can't go through this every time we meet someone new."

"It's not every time we meet someone, you know that. And you told me you believed me. If you don't, then why the hell did we move out here? I thought you understood—"

"I *do* understand, and I did believe you, but this is different. We aren't in the city any more."

"It's not different! There's something off about that man, I don't know what it is, but I can feel it. We have to stay away from him. If you believed me then, you have to believe me now."

"You haven't been having the dreams, have you?"

She shook her head.

"I'm just saying that maybe it's just something left over from living in Anchorage," George said. "But if it makes you feel better, I'll stay away from him."

"Thank you. And maybe you're right, maybe it's nothing. And no, I haven't had any dreams like before since we moved here. Perhaps I am overreacting."

George put his arm around her shoulders and they started to walk back to the house. "Don't worry, the past is behind us now. The darkness won't follow us here."

Anna turned her head and kissed him. "Let's just focus on our lives here. We have everything we want. You have the novel you've always wanted to write, and I have my painting. The only thing that can ruin this is ourselves."

Chapter 6

JAMES AND ELENA: DAY 3

Elena woke up with a feeling of great unease the next morning. She knew what she needed to do—it was the reason she was here after all, wasn't it, the reason she continued to stay. But now more than ever, she didn't want to go through with it. She dressed in her own clothes, newly washed and dried, and made her way downstairs. James was pouring beaten eggs into the pan. He looked so happy standing there, busily chopping the fillings for their omelets. She stood there and watched him before he glanced in her direction. A smile lit up his face as he said good morning. Elena forced a smile in return.

She was very solemn as they ate and it troubled James. He stopped eating and asked if there was something wrong.

"What? No, I'm fine." She quickly stuffed a forkful of egg into her mouth.

James frowned. "Elena, I can tell that something is bothering you. You can tell me what it is. I'm here for you."

"I think I just need some time on my own to sort through some things. I don't want to leave yet, but I think I need some fresh air and some time to think."

"Yeah, of course, I understand. Take as much time as you need."

Elena finished her omelet and dropped her fork onto the plate. "I'm going to take a walk. I might be gone for a few hours." She immediately got up from her chair, grabbed a backpack from the living room, and strode out of the house.

James remained sitting there, a little puzzled by Elena's behavior. He wished he knew what was troubling her, that there was some way to help. He thought about the house, and how he had ended up there. *What made me go down that dirt road? Did something happen to the previous occupants of this house? It was strange that the door would be unlocked, almost as if this place was waiting for me.* These thoughts were still going through his head when he decided that maybe he needed to get out as well.

So he walked down the path and stood on the shore. His thoughts were fleeting and chaotic. He thought about how everything seemed so different with Elena here. Yet somehow, at the same time, it felt as if nothing at all had really changed. James found himself thinking about her quite often, yet his feelings toward her were confusing.

Sometimes he felt like there was a connection between them, but then he questioned whether it was real, and wondered whether Elena felt anything for him at all. And then there was whatever she was going through. *Is that why I'm drawn to her? Because she's in distress and maybe I can help her? No, there's more to it than that. She's more than just a damsel in distress. But what was it that drove her to try to kill herself?*

With that thought, he was forced to examine his own situation. Why had he really gone up there? Would he really have jumped? Would it really have been him floating in the water if she hadn't jumped first, drowning, his spine broken? If he was being honest with himself, he knew the answer to these questions. He knew damned well why he was on that cliff. He knew what he would have done, and every little thing that had led him there.

James turned back and walked to the shed by the garden and pulled out a yellow sea kayak from its rack beside a matching red one. He had gone out several times before, and he felt that perhaps some time alone on the water would do him some good.

When he had paddled a good way out into the water, he stopped and let himself drift with the current. *Everything is different now*, he thought, rousing himself from a deep stupor. *Ever since I found this house, it's felt like reality has started to slip away from me. Now with Elena here it's like reality is even further away, and some strange dream has taken over. At any moment, I may wake up and find myself still standing on that cliff, looking down into those mesmerizing waves. But is this some kind of beautiful dream or something much worse? Maybe I don't want to find out the answer to that question.*

It seems funny to me, how people will always talk about certain things like they're an inevitability. Like finding that special someone to settle down with and have a family with is something that will just eventually happen. But then you start to realize that even if that's what you want more than anything, you might never be able to make that connection. After a while, you start to realize that love is far from inevitable, and you understand that perhaps it's that way with a lot of things. That you aren't the type of person where things like that are inevitable.

James sat there for a while, contemplating these and other thoughts that continued to flow through his head. The water was still, and he found some peace and beauty in the solitude and quietness of his surroundings. After a while, he paddled back.

As Elena walked along the shore, she tried to focus on her surroundings and shut out everything else. She could manage walking, just putting one foot in front of the other. *I just have to get to that chunk of driftwood*, she would tell herself. And then, *just have to get around the next bend*. Yes, walking was easy—thinking was what she didn't want to do, not right now. Thinking about James, about what she had to do, about how she had gotten into this mess in the first place, and thinking about—no, she couldn't think about that. So she kept on walking.

After Elena had walked several miles, tears suddenly came to her eyes. "Why did this have to happen to me? Why did any of this have to happen?" she asked herself out loud. "This wasn't supposed to happen like this. I wasn't supposed to ... to feel whatever I feel toward him. Now what am I supposed to do? Why did I have to meet that man? Why did *he* ever have to enter my life?"

She stopped walking, and looking out over the bay, she yelled out, "FUCK YOU, COLE! I hate you and everything you did to me! Why did you have to make me do this? I can't do this, not any more." Elena dropped to her knees, still weeping. "Why did any of this have to happen? Why does everything have to be so fucked up? I can't. I just can't do it; there has to be another way."

She sat there in the sand, wiping the tears from her face as her crying started to subside. Then she reached in the backpack and grabbed a pair of headphones, plugged them into her phone, and listened to music. She was glad the phone was waterproof and had survived the fall, if for no other reason than for the songs she had stored on it.

Elena stared across the bay and just let the music take away, at least temporarily, some of the pain and sorrow that she felt deep within her soul. The sea foam was being pushed up along the sandy shore by the constant waves, one being replaced by the next in only a moment. She looked across the water over to the mountains on the other shore, how big and majestic they looked, and how small and insignificant she felt sitting here in their presence. She wished that James had never pulled her out of the dark water that she had jumped into. That she would've been able to die there, that all of this would be over. That she would've found her final resting place in that darkness of water. Then she wouldn't have to struggle with all of the darkness in her life.

It was getting late, and it had started to rain when Elena finally got back to the house and went inside.

"There you are," James said from the living room. He was sitting on a couch with a book. "I was beginning to think you might have left, or something worse. When you said you might be gone for a while, I didn't think it would be the whole day. I already ate, but there's some leftover chicken in the fridge."

"I'm sorry," Elena said. "I didn't think I would be out so long either, but there were some things I had to work out in my head."

James noticed how sad she looked, slightly wet from the rain. "It's fine. I'll heat up the chicken for you."

After Elena finished eating, James got a fire going in the fireplace as Elena stared out the big bay window at the sheets of dark rain.

James went into the kitchen, and a minute later the teakettle was whistling. "Come over here and sit by the fire," he said as he walked back into the living room with a mug in each hand.

She curled up at the very end of the couch; her coiled legs between them while her face was distant and emotionless.

"You've hardly said a word since you got back," James said. "It's just ... I hate seeing you like this ... but I know you don't want to talk about it, not to me at least."

"Don't say it like that," Elena said, her voice rising. "There are some things that people have to deal with on their own. There is so much that you don't understand ... though I fear you will before the end. I would like to let you in, but I can't. I just can't."

"But you can. You just have to choose to trust me. We all have a dark side. We all do things we regret and know are wrong."

"And we all have secrets that we keep to ourselves. Parts of ourselves that we don't show other people, even those closest to us."

James stared into the fire for a while. "Maybe we should leave here. We could go tomorrow, drive far away. Maybe you just need a fresh start to get away from whatever is haunting you here."

"Yes ... *you* should. Get far away from here, far away from me. You should get away before it's too late. I'm no good for you," Elena said, starting to cry.

"Don't say that. I'm not going to leave you, not at a time like this. Don't put yourself down like that; I can see that you are good, so don't say that you aren't. I—"

"Don't!" She leapt off the couch and ran outside into the rain.

James went after her. She was standing on the end of the small rocky outcrop that extended from the shore. She was kneeling in the dark and he could hear her crying.

As James approached her he said gently, "Elena, I'm—"

"Leave me alone!" Elena shouted. "I don't want you here, please, just leave me alone," she said in a softer voice, weeping.

"No," James said gently, squatting down next to her. "I'm not leaving you. You being here, it's one of the best things that has happened to me in a while. When you're ready to talk, I'll be here, and until you're ready to talk to me, I'll still be here. Because I'm not leaving you, not when it's clear you need someone to help you through this."

Elena, still crying, looked up at James. There was still sadness in her face, but there was also gratitude, and perhaps something more. She looked back down at the wet rocks. They sat there like that until Elena seemed calm enough that James thought he should get her out of the rain. He touched her shoulder.

"Come on, let's go back inside," James said. "You'll catch a cold."

"Okay," she said softly.

James helped her up, and they slowly walked back to the house. When they got inside, the fire was low, so James restocked it with more wood.

"I'm going to change out of these wet clothes," Elena said.

"That sounds like a good idea, I'll do the same."

They went upstairs and into their respective rooms. James put on a new pair of jeans and a white t-shirt and waited for Elena downstairs. When Elena came down, she was wearing flannel pajama bottoms and a long-sleeve grey top.

"Let's forget about our troubles for tonight," James said. "Let's just sit and enjoy each other's company."

"Sure, I guess," Elena said.

"There's a bottle of wine; I think we could both use some." James left the room and then came back holding a bottle of red wine and two glasses. They sat on the couch in front of the now blazing fire, and James poured them both a full glass.

"... So to stop people from breaking into his car," Elena was saying, "he rigged it, I don't remember how exactly, to shock anyone who tried to break in." Her laughter started to overcome her words. "So one night he was woken up by someone screaming or yelling or something, and he said, 'Good, that'll teach 'em.'"

"That's ridiculous," James said, laughing.

"He was always telling crazy stories like that. I could never tell if they were true or not," Elena said, still laughing a little. She looked at her empty glass sitting on the table. "Well, I guess the wine's gone."

"Not to worry, there's plenty more where that came from."

"No, I didn't mean you had to get ..." Elena started to say, but James was already headed to the kitchen.

When James returned and poured them each another glass of wine, Elena took a sip and then looked at James. After a moment, she said, "Thank you."

"For what?"

"You know ... this, right here."

James smiled at her but didn't say anything. After a moment, he went to drink from his own glass. "So, tell me, what makes you happy?"

"Oh, I'm not even sure I really know any more. When I was a girl, it was easy, there were so many things I enjoyed back then and so few worries. I enjoy good company, I guess. Do you believe in absolute evil?"

James raised his eyebrows, surprised by the veer in the conversation. "I know that there is great evil and darkness in this world, and that some have been touched too heavily by it. And that there is also great goodness and light in the world for those who wish to look for it. I don't think that anyone is absolutely evil. I think everyone has some light inside of them, just like everyone also has darkness inside them as well."

"I have seen true evil, and darkness so thick it seems impossible to escape from it. Is it true that there is a light strong enough to penetrate it, or is some darkness too thick for even the strongest light?"

"I think light is always stronger than darkness, although it might not always seem like that's true."

James feared that the conversation was getting too dark again, and that Elena might fall into another depressive state. "Well, let's put on some music, shall we." He turned the stereo on and pressed play. The music that started to play was from a band called Daughter. James had heard it before, but in this moment he felt like it was the most beautiful and heartfelt melancholic music he had ever heard.

When he came back to the couch, Elena was looking at him, her eyes drawing him in. Eyes that were beautiful and yet mysterious, almost unsettling if he looked at them for too long. He thought he sensed something in the look she was giving him, desire maybe, but he couldn't be sure.

Longing, that's what he saw there, longing for ... something. What that something was, James could only guess—happiness, peace, to find something, to be found. He felt himself being drawn to her in a way unlike anything he had experienced before.

They sat together for a little while, not talking, just looking at the fire, listening to the music and occasionally sharing a meaningful glance. Then Elena got up and walked over to the fire. After a little while, still looking at the fire and feeling the buzz from the wine, Elena started to dance very slowly and gently to the music. At first, James just watched her. Elena was so beautiful, with the contrasting light and shadow from the flickering flame playing across her body. She started moving around a little more, sometimes looking at James and keeping her eyes closed other times. Then Elena gestured with her hand for James to come and join her.

James slowly got up, then started dancing across from her. They continued dancing like this, separately yet together. They were both wrapped up in a certain kind of feeling that was in the room. A feeling created by the music, the wine, the rain outside, and also some kind of connection that they shared with each other. A feeling of contentment, belonging, warmth. Elena grabbed James's hands, and they danced very close to each other. They stared into each other's eyes, a deep stare that they held for several seconds, one filled with emotion and longing.

Then Elena tripped on something—maybe her own feet—and fell onto the floor on her back. James fell with her, falling partially on top of her. He looked at her, and was about to kiss her, when Elena laughed a little and gently pushed him off. James started to laugh with her and simply felt happy to be in this moment with Elena by his side. They looked at each other, and Elena took his hand and smiled. Then she looked into the fire. There was a mesmerizing quality to it, and she felt very warm inside. She felt happy, happier than she had felt in a long time. Still lying there, Elena's eyes grew very heavy, and she slowly fell asleep lying next to James on the rug by the fire.

James stayed lying there for a while, looking at Elena as she slept. She looked so peaceful. He watched her breasts as they moved up and down with her breathing. His eyes moved over the rest of her body as he thought about whether he really would be able to be with her completely. About what it would be like to have sex with her, to make love to her.

It had been a long time since he had last felt this way about someone. It was almost six years since he had last seen Katie, and that was different than this. He had known that she didn't feel the same way about him; he had just refused to accept it until he had no choice but to accept that things could never work out. Now twenty-seven years old, he had begun to doubt that he would ever feel that way again, especially as he spent less and less time around other people.

But did Elena really feel the same way about him? And could he trust the feelings he had for this woman that he still hardly knew? He got up and brought a pillow from the couch and put it under Elena's head. Then he put a blanket over her and put another log on the fire. He sat down on the couch and fell asleep himself.

Chapter 7

GEORGE AND ANNA:
THREE MONTHS EARLIER

Anna woke up covered in sweat. She could feel her heart pounding in her chest. She rolled onto her back and concentrated on the swerving half-moons in the ceiling plaster. She lay there like that until the fear slowly started to leave her mind. To her left, she saw the vacant space in the bed next to her. Then she got up and walked toward the bathroom, glancing out the window to see that it was snowing again.

After splashing water on her face, Anna looked at herself in the mirror. She saw the dark circles under her eyes, the matted mess of black hair falling down from her head. "I don't know how much more of this I can take," she muttered. She made her way downstairs and when she entered the kitchen, the aroma of fresh black coffee hit her. Even just the smell of it rejuvenated her slightly. She poured herself a cup, breathing in the aroma before she took a sip. George was sitting at the table in front of the window reading a book, his own cup of coffee by his side.

"Do you remember how we just sat and watched the snow fall?" George asked, not lifting his head from his book. "It was the first proper snow of the season, the first snow at our new home."

"It's getting worse." Anna took a seat next to him, sipping from her coffee mug.

"It was only two months ago, yet it feels like it was much longer than that. The snow seemed more beautiful then, fresh and new, white and pure."

Anna remembered it well. It was one of the last wonderful days that she could remember. Only a week ago, they had celebrated the New Year, but it hadn't seemed like much of a celebration. Christmas wasn't much better. She had put on a cheerful face, and together they put on some semblance of a holiday spirit, but it was a charade that fooled neither of them. A wall of separation had already begun to cement itself between them. They still ate together, talked with each other—albeit mostly superficially—and still slept together. But she felt so alone, so distant. Now they both spent most of their time away from each other.

Putting away those thoughts, Anna continued on what she said before. "Maybe not worse, but it's certainly not getting any better."

George finally put the book down and looked at Anna. "I don't know what to say. Ann, you look like a mess." He ran his hand through her hair. "Did you drink any of that tea I gave you?"

"You know I can't stand that stuff, and it doesn't help anyway."

"I'm trying, you know. You said that if we moved out here you would be better, that—"

"And it was, for a while at least. I felt better than I had since we first met. That first month or two, it was truly wonderful. But now there's *him*, I can feel his presence in my dreams, I can sense his desires. I know it's *him*."

"You have to come off this. Cole is just a man, and there is nothing to indicate that he's evil. You're sick, that's all this is. I think you should think about seeing a doctor again—we'll find you a new one, of course."

"*Sick? Doctor?* I thought you believed me! You know what any doctor is going to do. Probably try to check me into a mental hospital, or at best just shove a bunch of drugs down my throat until I can't feel anything at all."

"I do believe you, but that doesn't mean that modern medicine can't help you. We had an unpleasant experience last time, but this time will be different. I care about you, Anna, and I just want to make sure you don't try to do something to yourself again."

"Do something to myself? You know why I took those pills. You didn't believe me; no one believed me. Even after it was proven that I was right all along about Vito Borgenson. And I know I was also right about that Kevin kid, and that woman, what was her name, Jessica. You had even said yourself that she seemed a little unhinged. But now it seems you've never believed me, even after that."

"I moved us out here, didn't I? I only ever wanted you to get better. Even if you really do get little glimpses into other people's minds sometimes, or something beyond what most people experience, you always took it to such an extreme and unhealthy place."

"That's because you never understood what it was like. You can never understand. I don't just see the evil inside of people, I *feel* it. I feel their dark desires as if they were my very own. And on top of that, to have no one believe you, not even your own husband. To feel absolutely alone, like maybe you really are going crazy, even though you know you're not. You start to find yourself in your own little world, a world that others can't enter, because they can't possibly understand what you're going through. After a while, maybe you can't take it any longer, and you only see one option in front of you. That is what you've never understood, and now I'm realizing that you never will. Worse, that you'll punish me because you can't understand." Anna pushed her chair back and walked out of the room.

After a moment, George threw his book against the wall. He got up and walked over to the door, put on his boots and winter jacket and went outside, slamming the door behind him.

Anna went upstairs to her studio. There were several paintings propped against the floor and walls, beautiful paintings of the bay, of the cottonwoods turning yellow, and even of their own house. There were several paintings off to one side that took on a decidedly darker tone. These were her more recent paintings, and there was a stark contrast between them and her earlier work. Dark landscapes of the night, still beautiful in their own right, yet there seemed to be some kind of darker presence hidden beneath the surface. In the center of the room, there was a large canvas set on an easel. Looking at it, she still found herself startled by what she had painted. It was almost finished now, and was perhaps her best work yet. But this was something darker, something that came from her dreams, dreams that were now filled with darkness and agony and despair. This was all she could seem to paint now. No more crystal blue bays or sun-kissed pines. Now there were only these images, ones that she never seemed able to shake from her mind.

A shiver went up her spine as she looked at it. But there was no denying that she had been turning out her best work these past several weeks. They were dark, sure, but the quality of the workmanship had reached a whole new level. It scared Anna to think about the source of her inspiration.

She had never spent much time painting people before, preferring to stick mainly to landscapes, but the detail that came out in the woman on the canvas in front of her was startling. The fear and despair that came across in her eyes, and the eroticism that still managed to come forth from her. It was unsettling, yet beautiful. Anna sat down in the chair and closed her eyes, letting the images from her dream come back to her. Then she opened her eyes again and picked up her brush.

Chapter 8

JAMES AND ELENA: DAY 4

Elena woke up still lying on the floor with the blanket pulled tight around her. She looked toward the fireplace where a few red embers were still burning away, then around the room to where James was asleep on the couch. As she looked at him, she got that warm feeling again. She wanted to go to him and wake him up. Instead, she decided to get some fresh air and went outside.

When James woke up, he saw an empty blanket and pillow where Elena had been sleeping. After walking into the kitchen for a glass of water, he looked out the window. Dawn was just breaking, and there was a thin fog over the water. He saw her standing on the tip of the rocky outcrop, the same place where she had run to the night before. As he approached her, she turned around to face him. The cloud of sadness and anxiety had come over her face once again.

"Good morning," he said. "I hope you slept well. I thought about moving you to the couch, but I didn't want to disturb you."

"Yes, I did. Last night was wonderful, but ..." Elena knew what she had to say, wanted to say, but didn't know how to say it. "But now we have to come back to reality."

"This is reality. You and me, right now, we are reality."

Elena shook her head. "You're still lost in the dark. Living in a dream that can never be real."

"Elena, this can still be real. Whatever it is you're fighting against, I can help you, you just have to let me."

"You think this is real? What is reality but your own perceptions? And when new information comes to light, doesn't that change what's reality to you? So then there are three different realities at play here, aren't there? My reality, your reality, and then the way things really are." Elena had been shifting her gaze back and forth between James and the ocean. Now she looked intently into his eyes. "I would love to live in this dream that we've created over the last couple of days; it's a very beautiful dream, but I can't keep living in a false reality. We all must wake up sometime and face reality."

James could tell that Elena was trying to tell him something. Maybe the truth about the darkness that was eating at her. This was what he had been waiting for, so he made sure to choose his words carefully, not wanting to scare her away from telling him. "It's true that new information changes one's perspective. But there are realities that are true and real within and of themselves. Though our perspective may change with new information, that truth and reality never changes. No matter what happens, that truth remains the same."

He paused to make sure that he had her full attention. "No matter what dream I've been living in," he said, looking into her eyes, "the way I feel about you is a reality that won't change."

"James, don't be naïve. How you feel about someone—about me—that can always change." Elena sighed heavily and ran her hands through her hair. "I want to tell you the truth, but some truths are just too difficult to put into words. Reality can be a dark and sad place. Sometimes you feel that you can never escape it." Elena looked at James and then froze. Fear came over her face. "What am I doing?" she asked herself softly. Then, after a short pause, she yelled out, "I can't do this, I'm sorry!" She turned and sprinted down the outcrop of rocks, then south along the shore, in the opposite direction from where she had gone the day before, away from the cliffs she had leapt from.

James started to run after her. "Elena! Wait, come back." Then he stopped. *Shit. I shouldn't have pushed her so much, now she may never open up to me. She was about to tell me something, maybe everything. I should've just waited until she was ready.* He turned around and looked across the water. James tried to think of what he should do. He thought of the last few days he had spent with her. He thought about how Elena had spent the previous day almost completely on her own, and then realized that maybe this wasn't the right time to leave her alone. That maybe she needed someone, even if she didn't want to talk. If she still wanted him to leave, he would leave. He ran after her.

He hopped across the stones that had been laid in the river, then slowed to a walk, wondering how far she had gone. The coastline was a little different over here, with the mountains much closer to the shore than where they had been farther north. The thought occurred to him that she might not have even stayed on the coastline, that she could've cut in between trees near the base of the mountain. A rush of relief passed through him when he rounded a corner and saw her a little ways off in the distance. She was on her knees looking down at the ground, her hair covering her face. As James got closer, Elena turned her head to look at him, then immediately looked away. She slowly got up and started to walk away, and then she stopped, still facing away from him.

"I'm sorry," James said as he approached her. "I should've never pushed you to tell me anything that you didn't want to share. You don't have to tell me anything."

Elena remained silent, her back still turned to him.

"I understand if you want to be alone, just ... come back to the house tonight. Don't leave, not yet." James turned and started to walk away.

"Wait."

James stopped. Elena slowly turned to face him, and he could see that her eyes were red and still wet from crying.

"Stay," she said. "I don't want you to leave."

"I won't."

Elena slowly walked over, put her arms around him, and rested her head on his shoulder. "I'm sorry, I just can't talk about it. I thought I could, but I just can't."

"Shhh, it's fine, you don't have to tell me anything if you don't want to." James said as he held Elena tight and ran his free hand through her hair.

"I just want to live in this moment a little longer. I want to be in this dream a little longer, before it all collapses and all I'm left with is darkness ... and death. I want to be with you, even if it's only just for a little longer."

Elena swayed gently against James. She was so grateful that he didn't have to know about the darkness that she was keeping from him. She couldn't risk losing him yet. Eventually, she would have to tell him the truth, but not yet.

As they were standing there, James heard a strange guttural kind of barking in the distance. He looked up and saw several sea lions lying on the large rocks that were rising out of the water. He turned so Elena was facing the rocks and pointed. "See, there's still beauty in this world."

Elena gave James a slight smile. Then she grabbed his hand and gently pulled him to follow her. They walked along the shore side by side, hand in hand. It was low tide, and they passed tide pools with starfish and sea anemones and rocks covered with barnacles.

After only a short while, Elena spoke again. "James, what were you running away from?"

"I'm not sure what you're talking about."

"When you quit your job and ended up at this house. What were you running from?"

James stopped walking and let go of Elena's hand. "I wasn't running away from anything."

"Hmm, let's see. You quit your job, you left your home and everyone you knew. You left what was safe, secure, and known, to drive all the way through Canada and up here to Alaska. Without a plan or a job, or any idea of what you were going to do, and with what I can only guess wasn't an enormous sum of money. Obviously, you were running away from something. That, or you were trying to run toward something. Either way, it's basically the same thing."

"Well, when you put it that way ... I don't know. I suppose, in a way, I guess I was running away from something. Or toward something, or both. I don't know if I even fully understood it myself. I guess it starts out as a feeling, and then slowly turns into a need. A need to find out if things can be different somewhere else. To see what else is out there in the world, and in the process find out more about yourself."

James had been pacing aimlessly about as he talked. He now looked at Elena as he continued. "So in the end, I guess it's not much more than trying to run away from a sense of meaninglessness and toward some kind of purpose that you still haven't found. It doesn't really work that way though, does it? If you move somewhere else, even get a different job, that doesn't change who you are. That doesn't fix the problems that you have with yourself. I kind of knew that even then, but still I had to leave. It's just what I felt like I had to do. I had to do something."

Elena studied his face, trying to see whether he was holding something back. "So that's it? You couldn't find fulfillment in your life, so you ran away?"

"Well, it's more than that, though. I was never able to relate to people like most people can. I'm not sure how to explain it exactly, but I spent most of my life alone because of it. In a lot of ways, that kind of life isn't that bad, and even in sadness there is beauty, but there's also a darkness to that kind of life as well."

"Life casts a shadow on us all, doesn't it? We all come from different backgrounds and go through unique experiences. From the moment we enter this world, we're all flawed and broken. We all fight and search for some meaning or purpose in this life. Most of us never find it. But whatever happens, I'm glad I met you, James. You helped me see that there's more than darkness in this world. Maybe we all need someone else to fix the broken parts of ourselves. That none of us are meant to be alone. But how rare it is to find someone that actually can truly make the other person better."

Elena fell silent and neither of them spoke for a while. They walked a little more and then Elena sat down on a rock. James was still walking about, looking at various shells half-buried in the sand.

"Do you think people can change?" Elena asked, still staring out over the bay.

"I don't know. I know that I have tried to change many times but was never able to. I think it's possible for some people to change, I guess, but by and large, most people never do. Why?"

"So you don't think I can change?"

"Elena, I wouldn't want you to change. I think you're good the way you are, even with the parts of yourself that may still be broken."

"That's because you don't know me. You only see what you want to see, and you've only known me for what, four days now. How could you possibly know me after such a short time?"

"I know enough," James said. "With the circumstances that we met in, the time we spent together. I know that you're a good person, someone who has been through more darkness than most people, but hasn't let that destroy the beauty that lies in your soul."

"Do you always see the best in people?"

"No, but I see the best in you."

Elena smiled slightly and joined him on his search among the detritus that had washed up on the shore—smoothed glass, seaweed, a dead fish. Then she stopped abruptly when she saw what looked like a small dead octopus that was washed up between the rocks. It only appeared to have three tentacles, and Elena couldn't help but think how strange it was to see it washed on up on the shore like this.

"We should probably start heading back," James said. "I don't know about you, but I'm getting pretty hungry, and thirsty too."

"Yeah, sounds good," Elena replied, still staring down at the remains of the octopus.

It was midafternoon now. Elena and James were back at the house. The sky outside was overcast, as it so often was, especially at that time of the year. It was the tail end of April and out on the Alaskan coastline, it always seemed to either be raining, or appearing like it wanted to rain. Elena was standing with her arms crossed in front of the big window in the living room and staring into the grey, expecting the rain to start falling at any minute. James came over and gently placed his hand on her shoulder.

Elena shrugged her shoulder away from his hand and then looked at him. "James ... there's something I have to tell you."

"Okay."

"I can't tell you everything, but ... when I was young everything was easy, simple. My childhood years were cheerful. I had dreams, I had plans, a vision of how my life would turn out. I was content, and tried to do what was right, what was good. But things never turn out how you expect them to. Somewhere along the way, I had veered off and went in another direction. Here, let's sit down."

They sat across from each other on either side of the coffee table near the fireplace. "I guess it mostly started when I was seventeen," Elena continued. "I was living in Anchorage, and started going out with this guy named Jeffrey. He seemed like he was a pretty good guy, attractive and funny. But I could tell from the beginning that he also had a harder side, an edge about him. I had a feeling, right from the beginning, that he would cause trouble if I stayed with him, but at the time I didn't care. I was restless with my life, and I wanted to do more, experience more, feel more, and I knew Jeff was the ticket. I told him I wanted to wait when the subject of sex came up, knowing that it was more than just a physical act, but it didn't take long for him to convince me otherwise. Jeffrey had this way about him in how he could get me to do things. Things that I would probably never have done otherwise.

"I moved in with him after I graduated from high school. Things seemed to be pretty good for a while, hanging out with friends and partying fairly often. But I was restless and unhappy with my life. I was getting fed up with Jeff and his unpredictable mood swings, which seemed to be getting more and more erratic. So when I found he was sleeping with other women, I left him. I was now on my own, and I decided I should get my life together, realizing that I was on a dead-end road. So I repaired my relationship with my mom, which hadn't been very good since I had left, and became real close with her again. My dad left when I was real young and I've never seen him since, so it had always been just me and Mom. I got a solid job and was looking into going to college. Then … then my mom died. It was a car accident."

Elena turned away from him and looked out the window. She wiped away a tear that was forming and noticed that there was now a steady rain outside. "It devastated me; I didn't know what to do. During this time of grief, I met Jeffrey again, and he said how sorry he was, how terrible he felt about the way he treated me. Seeing him again made me realize how much I had missed him, and forget about how he had betrayed me. We got back together, and I plunged back into my old lifestyle. I lost myself in drugs and any other distractions to keep from thinking about reality. Soon I didn't care if Jeffrey was still sleeping around any more, as I started to do the same.

"I was twenty-five now and I hated what I had become. I wanted the girl that used to be me back, but it was too late. I could never be that innocent girl again with nothing but hopes and dreams of what the future held. This hate for myself drew me all the more towards drugs, chasing that high, trying to escape the reality that I was in. Anything to take the pain and sadness away, even if it was just temporary. I had a full-fledged meth addiction by this point and spent all my money on getting that next fix. It became so bad that I even started sleeping with my drug dealer when I ran out of cash."

Elena got up from her seat, not able to sit still any longer, and walked back over to the window. "I guess I could try and say that I just fell into the wrong crowd, that other people made me into who I became. And while that may be partially true, the fault is mine and mine alone. I made the choice to wander down this path, because part of me wanted to choose this path. This world I fell into and became part of was a dark world, filled with people that only take and never give. They take and take until there's nothing left. When you're in that world, though, it's the only world you know. The drugs give you a temporary release from that dark reality, but when that feeling dissipates, you feel even emptier than before. The sex was the same, there was never any genuine love associated with it. When I was at a very dark place; emotionally and physically, someone came to me, and ..."

Elena broke off as she started to cry. "I'm sorry, I hate that part of my life. I would erase all of it if I could, but it's all part of who I am and I can never go back and change that. It's also the road that eventually drove me into the water that you saved me from." She was sniffling and wiping the tears from her face as they continued to fall. "I told you ... I told you I wasn't a good person. You have every right to hate me."

"Don't say that," James said. "Elena ... what you shared, I know it wasn't easy to tell me all that. Whatever you did in the past, that's the past. It isn't who you are now. I know you well enough to know that you're not like that anymore. The woman who stands in front of me right now, there is so much light and goodness inside that person. I can see it, it wasn't destroyed. Yes, there is darkness there too, but you have overcome it. I believe that what you experienced and have gone through, it has only made you stronger, even if you're still too broken right now to see it yourself."

This only made Elena weep all the more as she turned away from him again, not wanting him to look at her in this state any longer. James came up and squeezed her tightly in his arms.

"It's okay, I'm here. I'm here for you," he whispered in her ear.

"But what if it's not? What if it's not okay?" Elena turned around in his arms and faced him. "What if despite all of our best efforts, nothing turns out right? What if the only thing that awaits us is darkness?"

Before Elena could go through any more what-ifs, James kissed her gently on the lips.

At first Elena welcomed it, leaning into the kiss. Then her mind flashed to being somewhere else—with someone else. She was in another room; it didn't take her long to recognize it. She noticed the flowing red curtains out of the corner of her eye. She smelled that all too familiar cologne that *he* had always worn. Then she saw *his* face.

Elena shoved him away from her. "No!" she yelled as James stumbled back into the window. Coming back into reality, she saw that it was James that she had pushed away, in the midst of something that should have been a beautiful moment, a moment that she had been waiting for.

"Oh shit ... James, I'm sorry." Breaking down in tears all over again, Elena rushed to the far corner of the room, wishing that she could just disappear. She crouched down on the floor with her back toward James.

James was trying to get over the shock of being shoved into the window with quite some force. *Well, that's not exactly how I expected that to go.* He slowly walked over to the huddled and weeping mass that was Elena. "Elena ... are you okay? I'm sorry, I shouldn't have—"

"No, you didn't do anything wrong. It's me, it's all me, it's all my fault." After a pause, Elena looked up at him. "I'm sorry, I wanted to, I really did. It's just ... I'm fucked up, James, I am."

"No, don't say that." James crouched down next to her. "Its fine, we don't have to do this. Nothing needs to happen here."

"But I really did want to kiss you. It's just, something from before came to the surface right then. I saw ... *him*. I wish I could get it all out of my head, but I'm still all messed up."

"Saw who? Who did you see—"

"It doesn't matter, don't worry about it." Then, after a short pause, Elena continued in a different and somewhat hurried tone. "James, maybe we can try it again." There was a desperate tone in her voice that grew stronger as she kept talking. "I won't push you away this time. I'll be okay, I'll be fine. I can do it; I want to do it."

"No," James said in a calm yet stern voice. He sat down with his back against the wall. "Don't try to force something that isn't there. Maybe it's better this way. Maybe we aren't meant to be anything more than friends."

Elena was trying to wipe her tears away with the heels of her palms. "But you don't understand, I do want this, it's just that there's stuff ... shit that's still too fresh to get past right now, more than what I've told you just now. I just need some time to move past this."

"That's what I'm talking about, though. Whatever this is that you're going through, it seems pretty clear that you aren't ready to move on to whatever this is between us. I think that you—maybe us both—are too confused right now to know what we really want. To know if this is really real, or just some superficial feeling. Look, I'm not going anywhere, but I think that for now at least, we remain being just friends."

"And that's what you want?"

"What I want … what I want doesn't matter. I care about you, Elena, and I would like to help you if I can. What I want … is to do the right thing, to make a difference, to matter."

As Elena was trying to fall asleep, lying in her bed that night, she couldn't stop thinking about what had happened. About how James kissed her, and how she reacted. She hated herself for pushing him away. Why did all that shit have to come to the surface at the absolute worst time? It scared her how much she realized she had wanted that kiss to happen, how much she had started to feel toward him. *Maybe it's best that I reacted the way I did.*

As she kept shifting around in the bed, trying to find a position where she could sleep, she heard something fall to the ground. She got up and looked under the bed. It looked like a book. She sat on the bed with it and turned on the lamp. It was a small red leather-bound notepad. It must have been tucked between the headboard and the wall. She opened it to the first page, where there was a rough sketch of a house. It was roughly drawn but seemed to have a dark and threatening quality about it. It almost seemed familiar to Elena somehow, but she soon dismissed that thought. Turning over the page, she began to read the writing that was written there.

I saw the house again, as I often have. It was dark and shrouded in shadow. Fear and pain which I could viscerally feel emanated from it. I wanted to run away, get as far away as possible, but instead I went inside. I felt ropes burn into the skin of my wrists. I struggled against them, but could not escape. There were red curtains on the window, and I could feel the silk sheets under my skin. I could feel the fear, the fear that turned to sheer and stark panic when I saw him. A man standing at the foot of the bed. His face was all black, shrouded in shadow. Yet somehow I knew, I knew it was him.

On the next page was another roughly drawn sketch, that of a man in a suit standing tall and ominously. There was a flurry of pencil lines where his face was supposed to be, leaving nothing more than a black hole, a blank face. She turned the page again.

The next thing I knew, water surrounded me. I tried to lift my head, but something was holding me down. I couldn't escape the water. The icy chill stunned me as I struggled for breath. Just as I started to feel the sensation of death approaching, I was suddenly pulled from the water. I could only see a blur of light and shadows, and then I heard a voice. It was far away and muffled, yet I could make out most of what it said.

"This'll teach you. Why'd you do it? It didn't have to be like this, you know. None of this had to happen. This is your doing."

Then I felt myself being plunged into the ice cold water once more. I felt myself struggle until I couldn't struggle any more. Soon I was still, and everything went dark.

That was when I woke up.

Elena flipped past an empty page and onto what seemed to be a separate and new entry into whatever this was.

I walked into a room. It was dark except for the small amount of light from a bedside lamp. I could feel emotions, dark and horrific emotions that I knew were not my own, yet I felt them as if they were. I wanted to run from them, but instead I walked up to the bed. I could feel the want, the uninhibited desire I felt for the woman sleeping in that bed. Her long almond colored hair cascading over her shoulders. One of her breasts bare, uncovered by the sheet on top of her. She lay there sleeping, unbound, for there was no reason to keep her restrained in this room. I felt the feeling of being able to have her, to take her. She was mine now; I had her now, all to myself, and I could do whatever I wanted. As I stood beside her, I took a moment to take in her beauty. Then I felt myself leaning down and kissing her on her lips. She opened her eyes, and the fear that I saw in her eyes when she looked at me was unlike anything I had ever seen in another person. She tried to pull away, but I quickly grabbed hold of her.

I could now feel my own mind try to find its way into this dream and try to pull itself out of it, and back into the real world, at least my real world. I finally found myself able to enter my dream, or nightmare, and I screamed out, "Get out of my dreams! I don't want you here. Get away from me, Cole!" Then I was able to wake up.

Elena closed the notebook, not able to read any more. *Cole? No, it can't be.*

But of course it was. It made sense in some strange and incomprehensible way. These notes had to have been written by either Anna or George, most likely Anna. And

Cole, why not? He had been the source of Elena's own nightmares, so why would it be strange that he was the source of George and Anna's as well?

Elena looked down at the notebook once more. *Poor Anna, if this is really from you. What did you go through? What happened to you?*

Chapter 9

GEORGE AND ANNA: TWO MONTHS EARLIER

Anna woke in the middle of the night in a cold sweat. *Just a dream. No, this was too real, like all the others I've had. Will they ever stop?* She reached over and turned on the bedside lamp, and then picked up the notebook and a pen. A few nights ago, she had had the idea of writing these dreams—or whatever you could call them—down on paper. She thought that maybe if she put them down on paper she would be able to get them out of her head. It didn't seem to be working so far, but yet she did find the process to be somewhat calming. And sleep seemed to come on a little easier for the rest of the night. It occurred to her that this really wasn't that different from how she would paint during the day. Anna thought back to when George had seen some of her artwork the previous day.

Anna had walked into her studio to find George staring intently at her most recent work. George slowly turned around when he heard her enter. His gaze was hard, intense and searching, but he didn't say anything.

"I can't paint like before. I wish could, but I can't," Anna finally said. She waited, and when George still said nothing, she continued. "Sometimes I feel like I'm drowning in my own mind, a mind that seems to be filled with sadness, loneliness ... despair. I'm filled with vivid and stark images that come unbidden into my mind, dark images filled with shadow. But these images, they come to life beneath my brush, and when I finish I'm almost amazed by what I've created. Whether it's the dark waters swirling below a cliff, or a path through a hauntingly mysterious forest at night, or ... a house sitting atop a hill shrouded in shadow, as if it's keeping darker secrets inside. And then I'll be painting something else, a man with a black suit and tie, but you can't see his face because it's hidden in shadow."

Anna looked at the portrait sitting on the stand. "Another evening, a different image sticks with me so strongly that I'm soon putting it onto canvas as well. A woman, strikingly beautiful with long dark brown hair, lying on the floor." She was describing the painting that they were both looking at, one of a woman wearing a white tank top with her hair partially covering her face, though you could still see her eyes. "It's in the eyes. All the emotion comes across through her eyes. You can see the subdued fear that has turned to numbness and resignation. The sadness and loss of hope in her face, which comes across so vividly that it makes your heart break, but strangely you also find something hauntingly beautiful about her as well. Am I right?"

"They're all quite ... I mean the quality of the work is outstanding," George finally said. "In fact, they probably are your best work yet, but ... I worry for the mind that created them. There's some dark presence alive within it, and the way I can almost feel myself being drawn right into the landscapes is almost frightening. With the portraits, I can feel the emotion coming out from the canvas, and I find a kind of dark erotic beauty in them, even though I don't want to. Are all of these inspired by ... your dreams?"

"They aren't just dreams, not random abstract images. They're more than that. I know that they are real, the forests are real, the man with a blacked out face is real, and that woman is real. And knowing this reality and not knowing how to do anything about it, it's horrible. It makes me start to believe that the dark world of my dreams is more real than this one. It's similar to like before, in the city, but back there I would feel many people's emotions and feelings all battling for a place in my head, and sometimes I was able to drown them out somewhat. Here, I can only feel him and no one else, except for the pain and suffering of those women who also find their way into my dreams."

"Well, I wish you still painted like before, but at least you have an outlet—"

"And what about your book?"

George's eyes narrowed. "Of course you would bring that up. You can never just leave well enough alone, can you? You know I haven't been able to write, but you still have to twist that knife. You just can't help rubbing it in!"

"How do I know anything about what's going on with you any more? I don't see you for most of the day, and when I do we hardly say anything of substance. So how would I know that you haven't been able to write?"

"Yeah, well, don't forget that it was you who insisted on moving out here. That everything would be so much better. That you just needed to get away from the city. So don't blame me if things aren't the way you dreamed they would be."

"That's right, blame me," Anna said. "Everything is always my fault, isn't it? Well, since I'm obviously such a burden, I'll leave you alone so you can continue to spend all your time outside doing whatever the fuck it is you do."

Anna stormed out of the room. She crossed the hallway and fell onto her bed, tears coming to her eyes as she wished that George would come and console her, like he would have done long ago. But she knew he wouldn't.

Anna put the notebook back, then looked at the empty space next to her in the bed. He hadn't slept there last night, and she took a moment to wonder how long it would be before he would be there again, or if she even cared any more. Lying there on the bed, she had a feeling that things would only continue to get worse.

The following night, Anna was walking along the shore. It was approaching midnight, but the moon above illuminated the surrounding landscape. Walking at night was something that Anna had recently started doing, and she found that she actually quite enjoyed it, even in the coldness of winter. She could hear the movement of gentle waves to her right, the crunch of snow beneath her boots. There was something about the night. The world seemed different when it was shrouded in darkness, more disconnected from the reality that you felt during the daytime. There was a time when she would've been frightened by it, all the shadows of things not fully seen, and of what could lurk behind them. But now she felt as though she was part of the night. The darkness had claimed her, taking over her mind with dreams and thoughts that were not her own, and now she found comfort in the soft shadows of the night. As she walked, her mind found a degree of peace, even if it was only temporary.

Some distance ahead of her, she saw a smear of light appear. It was a fire on the shore near the house. For an instant she thought that the house might be on fire, then realized that the flickering light was too close to the water's edge. But why would there be a fire? Anna started to walk faster, anxious to find out the reason for it.

George was throwing something into the fire. At first, she thought it was a sheet of plywood, and then fear and anger jolted through her body as she realized what he was burning.

"George? George, what are you doing?" Anna yelled as she broke into a run. George grabbed another painting. "No! Stop it!" She saw the face of the woman she had just painted flash across her vision as George threw the canvas into the flames. "What the fuck, George? What are you doing!"

"I'm destroying it. I'm getting rid of all of it," he said, his voice angry yet calm.

"You can't. That's all of my work, everything I've done these past months. What are you thinking? What gives you the—"

"It's bad, Anna. It's unhealthy, these things that you paint, and it has to stop. I can't stand having you spend all day dwelling on this darkness."

"Burning my art won't help. I wish it could, but it doesn't work like that. I thought you understood that by now. Don't you think that I'd like to paint sun-drenched landscapes again, full of light and life? But these darker images now consume my mind, and painting them onto canvas is the only way I know to at least somewhat get them out of my head. They're the only outlet I have to keep myself sane. It's all that I have, and now you've burned it all away! Fuck, George, what the hell were you thinking?"

"I had to do something, something has to change. We can't keep going on like this."

"You had to do something! You did the one thing that would make things even worse! You're right, we can't keep going on like this, but I don't think we can ever come back from this. Where we are now, this house, this was our Plan B, this was our last resort. There's no fix any more, there is no getting better. This is all there is now, and it's fucked." Anna walked swiftly toward the house.

"Where are you going?"

"I'm going to find the manuscript of your book and burn that as well."

"Don't bother, that was the first thing I threw into the fire."

"Whatever," Anna said, and continued on into the house.

Five minutes later, she came out again, this time with several large picture frames in her arms. "What are you doing?" George asked her as she came up to the fire.

"You said you were getting rid of it all, right? Well, then we should get rid of these too. These people aren't who we are any more." Anna threw the photographs into the fire one by one.

They stood there in silence, watching the fire burn down. Then Anna looked over at George, waiting for him to return her gaze. When he finally met her eyes, it took her a moment to say anything. "I guess that's it then," she finally said.

"Guess so."

Anna turned and started walking slowly back toward the house.

"Anna," George called out. She paused, her back still to him.

"I'm sorry," he said.

It's much too late for that, she thought, but didn't say anything to him.

Several days later, Anna was walking along the shore. She usually preferred walking through the woods, but the snow was fairly deep now, and she didn't feel like trudging through it, even with snowshoes. But on the edge of the shore, the high tide had cleared it away. She tried to take in the beauty of nature, breathing in the crisp winter air. She gazed at the snowy mountains across the bay, and the spruce trees off to her side, their branches weighted down with snow. But she wasn't able to feel any of it, only the heavy weight that was pressing down on her mind.

She wasn't too far from the house when something started to draw her toward the woods. It was a subtle feeling, one that did not reach her conscious mind. So, without giving it a thought, Anna walked into the woods, trudging through the two or three feet of snow.

Soon she came upon a set of footprints. Knowing they had to be from George, she followed them. She hadn't gone very far when she heard what sounded like voices up ahead.

"... just staring out into the ocean. Sometimes she'll be like that for more than an hour at a time," George was saying. "I just don't know what to do any more. I feel like I might have lost her."

"I wish I could do more to help, but if her delusions have manifested themselves onto me like you say, there's not much I can do directly."

No, no, this cannot be, Anna thought. *It's not him, it can't be him.* Anna stopped behind a tree at the edge of the clearing in front of her. A large tree had fallen over a stream running through the open snow, and sitting on that fallen tree were two people, one of whom was George. The other was Cole.

"You've already helped a lot," George said. "I think I'd go crazy out here if I didn't have anyone else to talk to other than Anna, who I can hardly ever even talk to any more."

"She needs help, real help," Cole said. "Modern medicine has come a long way. You need to have her see a doctor, even if she doesn't want to. Leaving everything behind and moving out here, because that's what she felt she needed, that shows real dedication and love. Most people wouldn't go to such extreme lengths, but obviously it isn't working. She might hate you at first, but she'll come around to see the love you obviously still have for her. And I'll always still be here, even if it's just to be someone to talk to."

Anna's head spun. She took several steps back, stumbled, and fell into the snow. Images flashed through her mind. A hideous grin on Cole's face. Someone screaming, a woman falling to the ground. Blood splashing onto the grass. Someone falling from a cliff. Suddenly she felt the sensation of falling herself, falling through the air.

Then she saw the sky through the leafless branches of the trees. Anna scrambled to her feet and started to make her way back the way she had come. She tripped and fell several times before making her way out of the woods and back to the shoreline. She felt woozy, sick to her stomach, and anger was boiling deep within her. A feeing of such hurt, such betrayal cut through to the depths of her core, and from none other than her own husband, the one person who she thought was still there for her. *How could he? He said he would never see him again. And now they're ...friends! And they're talking about me! About things I only ever talked about with George! How could he confide in him? The one person I said he has to stay away from, the one I tried to tell him was evil? He never believed me, and now he's betrayed me, hurt me in a way that he will never understand.*

Anna stood on the shore, still and motionless as stone. She looked across the bay, and even past the mountains on the other side. Gazing beyond the physical world and out into something else, into what was beyond the fleeting world. She looked up into the sky, at the sun that was now shining between the many clouds. Then she looked down into the water in front of her. She let all the emotion and anger dissipate from within her, let it simply drift out of her and into the receding tide. A thin smile came onto her lips as she thought how beautiful it all was. In this moment, everything around her suddenly seemed beautiful. She started to laugh a little, because she no longer cared. Nothing seemed to matter any more.

Anna slowly walked to the water. The gentle waves first rolled over her feet, and then against her legs. The water was ice cold, but by now her mind was mostly disconnected from her physical being, and she hardly gave the sensation any notice.

The water was now past her waist and she was still staring out into the horizon when she thought she might have heard a voice behind her. The voice seemed very distant, as if traveling through some deep canyon from some other space and time. Whatever it was, she ignored it. She kept walking until the water had submerged her entire head. Then she stood still, looking through the water, seeing nothing. The world around her started to go black. As the darkness wrapped itself around her and began to take her away, she thought she felt something pulling her in another direction, but her world had already gone dark.

She was faintly aware of herself coughing, or maybe puking, she wasn't sure. She made out a blurry image of a face above her. It seemed as if it might be saying something, but she couldn't make out what. Then her world went black again.

Anna felt some sort of glow around her as she started to regain consciousness once more. When her vision cleared, she saw a blazing fire in front of her. She then realized that she was lying on a rug on the living room floor with multiple blankets covering her.

"Thank God you're okay," George said, who was sitting right next to her. "I was so worried. I thought I might have really lost you this time."

I think maybe you have. Anna wasn't sure whether she had only thought the words or actually muttered them out loud. Either way, George didn't seem to notice.

"I love you, Anna. You know that, right?"

"Yes, I know. But you don't believe me. You don't trust me." Then her eyes closed again and sleep took over once more.

Anna thought she might have felt herself drift in and out of wakeful consciousness a few times, but the next time she was fully aware of where she was, she found herself in the passenger seat of their car. She felt a hand tighten around her own and looked over to see George. "Where are we going?" she found herself asking.

"We're going to get you some help. Everything will be all right, I promise," George said.

"You can't help me, no one can." She looked out her window at the passing trees. She thought she heard him say something, but sleep was taking her away again.

Chapter 10

JAMES AND ELENA: DAY 5

Elena woke up the next day feeling slightly more optimistic about the future. James seemed to still accept her, even after knowing more about her past. But was she really able to tell him everything? She remembered the notebook she had started to read last night and grabbed it from the nightstand. She flipped through the pages. There were several more pages she hadn't read, and then the rest were blank. There was a drawing that caught her eye, and she quickly flipped back to it. It was a simply drawn map, but as Elena looked at it, a shiver ran down her spine. It looked eerily similar to something she had seen before. She didn't know why it was written in this notebook, but she knew exactly where it led. Elena flipped back to the last page of writing.

My dreams have shown me the way. I now understand what I must do.

Anna Green.

Elena wanted to show it to James, but she wasn't sure if it was the right time to do so. She was worried that it might open up too many questions, and also that she might have the answer to too many of those questions, answers that she wasn't ready to give. Elena put the notebook into her back pocket anyway. She made her way downstairs and saw James looking out the window while drinking coffee from his mug. He turned around when he heard her approaching.

"Good morning! There's still some coffee left if you want any," James said.

Elena sat down and ate some cereal and drank some coffee. James joined her.

"So what do you think happened to George and Anna?" James asked.

"Does it matter?" Elena replied, looking down at the cereal still in her bowl. "Their story is over, there's nothing we can do for them. Whatever happened to them ... I'm sure they're both dead now." Elena's mind drifted back to Anna's notebook. To how Anna mentioned Cole, and what that might mean.

"We don't know that. They could easily be alive and well, and there still might be something we can do, even if it's just to learn the truth. We're in their house after all, we owe them—"

"Owe them? Owe them what, neither of us ever knew them. If they're dead, we don't owe them anything, and

I'm telling you that they are dead." Elena looked up at James, a tear forming in her eye. "There are no happy endings, James. There was no happy ending for George and Anna, and there won't be any happy ending for us either."

"Why would you say that? This isn't about George and Anna, is it? So tell me, why do you keep talking like we don't have a future together?"

There was a moment of silence. "What are you keeping from me, Elena?" James asked, louder and more aggressively than he intended to.

"Don't." Elena abruptly got up, her chair making a grating noise against the floor. She pulled the notebook out from her pocket and threw it onto the table in front of him. "I found this behind my bed—Anna wrote it. Maybe it will tell you what happened to them." And then, without a moment's more hesitation, she stormed out the door.

"I'm sorry," James called out as the door slammed shut. He looked at the leather-bound notebook, then slowly picked it up.

Elena walked straight out toward the water's edge, then turned right to continue walking along the shore. "Oh God, why does everything have to be such a terrible mess?" she said while looking out into the sky. She sat down on a rock and rested her chin on her hands. A little while later, she noticed James walking in her direction. Instead of acknowledging him, she just continued looking out over the water.

"What's written in that notebook, it's all rather disturbing, and the dreams seemed to be very visceral," James said. "Yet it still doesn't really show what happened to them. But I know that this isn't about them, and I'm sorry. I know I said before that you didn't have to tell me anything you didn't want to, but whatever this is, it's a cloud that is hanging over you, over us." James made sure he was talking very calmly as he continued. "I think that it's time that you get this ... whatever it is you've been keeping from me, that you get it off your chest. Then we can get past it. You can trust me. I won't judge you. I might even be able to help you through it. Please, Elena, give me a chance."

Elena's emotions were all over the place, though the anger at her center was a constant. But as she looked into James's eyes, she found something very comforting in the way he was looking at her.

"I'm sorry," she said. "I know I have to tell you the truth. I'm just afraid that everything we have here will fall apart, that it will all be over, and that you'll hate me."

"You know I could never hate you—"

"Stop it, James, you know that isn't true. You took me out of my dark and sad reality for a little while and I'm so grateful for that, but I've still been lying to you this whole time. Just understand that I'm going to tell you the truth because of how I feel about you."

James waited for Elena to continue. She hopped up off the rock and paced the sand, agitated. It was obviously very difficult for her to say the words she was trying to summon.

"Fuck," Elena said. "Why does this have to be so difficult?" She stopped pacing and looked at James, suddenly perfectly still. The look she had on her face was almost that of anguish. "I never tried to kill myself," she said.

A moment of silence passed between them. A silence so thick that James almost couldn't breathe. Then she continued, speaking slowly so that it would all sink in. "At the cliff, when I jumped into the water. I jumped in to save you, James."

"What? But you said ..." Confusion and shock came over James's face as he tried to make sense of what she was saying. "But I jumped in to save you, you jumped in first. I don't under—"

"I jumped in first because I knew that you would try to save me. By jumping in first I prevented you from trying to kill yourself, because it forced you to save me instead."

"But—"

"James!" Elena said. Then in a much softer voice, "Please, just don't say anything until I'm done with what I have to say. I know you have questions, but it will be easier if you have all the information first." She paused for a moment. "Maybe I should start at the beginning. Well ... shit, why can't I think of the right way to tell you this. How do I describe what led me further down this horrible path?

"He said he just wanted to help me," she continued after another pause. "And that there was something special about me. His name was Cole, and he got me off the streets. Not only that, but he also helped me to get clean. At first I just thought he wanted to sleep with me, and to be honest, at the time I wasn't really against the idea, but he never made any advances while I was getting clean. He was handsome, but there was something off about him, although I couldn't place what it was. What really mattered was that he had saved me from the world I had found myself in. I looked up to him and was very grateful toward him.

"He brought me back to a big house, more like a mansion, an old and beautiful house in the woods on the side of a mountain. There was nothing else around except for the trees and the bay down below. Just me and Cole. I thought it was strange that I would be the only one up there with him, but I shook this eerie feeling off pretty quickly and focused on all the positives. I was finally off the streets, off the drugs, and I was finally getting better. He was kind and patient while I was going through withdrawals, and I grew more fond of him.

"You have to understand that I was at a very dark place when Cole came along, so there was almost a sort of indebtedness that I felt towards him for saving me from that life. After I was doing well and detoxed from the drugs I had been on, I remembered the person who I was before. And I started to realize that maybe Cole wasn't the man I thought he was. The way he acted sometimes, the things he would say, or wouldn't say. He would be very moody at times, and then in an instant—as if flipping a switch—he would be incredibly happy and nice. It was disturbing.

"It was around this time that he made his move on me. I knew this moment was coming, so it did not surprise me when he invited me into his room one night. Why else would he have brought me up there, if not for that? I had never thought he was helping me purely out of the goodness of his heart. In my experience, nothing ever comes for free. I was very grateful for everything he had done for me, and even though I had begun to sense that this man was not what he had appeared to be, I still wasn't against the idea of sleeping with him."

Elena started to pace again. "When he took me to his bed, it started out slow, and as we were kissing it was actually very nice. But then, as I was lying naked on his bed, there was something about the way he touched me that suddenly made me feel very cold. Any sense of desire or pleasure that I might have been feeling was suddenly very distant, and I found myself wanting more than anything to be somewhere else, anywhere else. As I looked into his face, what I saw scared the hell out of me. I don't know how to describe it, but looking into his eyes, all I could see was darkness. It was like the mask had come off and I could see who he really was. I could see the evil inside him. Before I even realized what I was doing, I said no, and then I yelled at him to stop. He did stop, and then I told him that I just didn't think I could do this right now. He smiled—a hideous smile—and I realized that I'd just made a big mistake, that no one says no to Cole. He slapped me across the face, then he climbed on top of me. I tried to fight him off, but after a brief struggle he forced his way into me with his hands around my throat. Then ... fuck."

Elena turned away from James. With tears in her eyes, she looked out into the horizon, her arms crossed. "When I was still on the streets I hated what I had become, so when Cole came and took me out of that world, I thought I was going back into the light." She laughed bitterly. "After that first night, he continued to force himself on me every night. After the first few times, I stopped resisting. I would just lay there and let him do his thing, hoping that he would eventually get bored and leave me alone. After he had his way with me for the night, he would leave, then keep me locked up in that room. He only ever let me out to go to the bathroom, and when we would have dinner together at night. He would talk a lot, about anything from books and their different themes to the current affairs of the world. I was always under his constant supervision when I was outside of my room. He said he was sorry, but he couldn't trust me any more. He said he didn't want to do this, but I was an ungrateful bitch for rejecting him after everything he had done for me. That it would have to be like this until I got my mind right again.

"One day when he seemed to be in a good mood, I asked him when I would be able to leave. 'Why would you want to leave?' he asked. 'No, you are the one for me. We belong together.' He told me that there had been many other women who stayed here before me, sometimes several at the same time. But he said how that was all over now. That things were different now, and we didn't need anyone else. I tried to make it clear to him I didn't want to stay, to make him see that things could never be what he hoped for with me. But he only got angry and locked me back in my room."

James watched her, not saying anything, concentrating on holding his body and expression still so he wouldn't distract her. It was clear she was having a hard time saying all of it. Her voice quivering from time to time, the agitated movements of her body.

"That night he never came into my room," she continued. "At first I was grateful, but he didn't show up the next morning either, or that afternoon. Nothing to eat, nothing to drink, nowhere to go to the bathroom. I worried that he might never come back and I would end up dying in there. When I heard the key turn in the lock that night, I was both relieved and frightened. When I saw that he didn't have any food with him, I knew why he had come. I had to do something, I couldn't take it any more. I grabbed a marble statue off the desk without him seeing, and as he approached, I tried to bash him in the head with it. But just before it connected with his forehead, he grabbed my wrist and twisted it until I let it go. Then he hit me and shoved me against the wall, yelling, 'Fucking bitch. If I can't be with you, nobody can.' I thought he was going to kill me. I could see the anger seething through him as he stared at me. I was so scared, but then he let me go and stormed out of the room.

"In the morning he came in again, this time calm and poised. He let me out and I was finally able to eat and drink something again. Water had never felt so vitalizing, and food never tasted so good before. I was still inhaling it when he told me that he wasn't going to hurt me, that things obviously hadn't worked out between us. He said I could leave, but if I did, there was still a debt that I needed to pay. James, he wanted me to bring you to him. He said someone has to die. I can either bring him you, or ... he would kill me. And if I tried to run, others would die as well. That's why I was watching you. That's why I jumped in first. It was only to save your life for a darker purpose."

Elena shuddered. Tears were heavy on her cheeks. "I'm sorry, I can't keep going. It's just too difficult to say any more right now. But you were different. He said you deserved to die, but you don't. You are everything that Cole's not. You're something I never thought that I would find. So I can't hand you over to the fate that Cole has for you, but I also can't leave. I can't run and leave others at the risk of his malice either. There is no good choice here." She was raising her voice now. "No matter what I do, no matter what I choose, everything is shit. There's no way out of this madness!" She paused momentarily and then said in a quieter voice, "I wish he would've just killed me and left everyone else out of this. It's what I deserve. I'm not a good person."

James couldn't stand watching her like this, but after all that he had heard, he didn't know what to say. Conflicting emotions were flooding through him. *How can this be true? How could she lie to me like this? Or could this fantastical story really be true? Has this all been fake, the way I thought she might have felt about me, and therefore the way I feel about her? Is any of it really real?* But the way she was standing there, crying, broken, and vulnerable, he knew that his feelings for her were as strong as ever. Or were they? In his confused state, he couldn't tell. He was unable to say anything, struck dumb by what he had just heard.

"Well, say something!" Elena yelled, still sobbing. "Say anything! Tell me you hate me, tell me to leave, tell me that you wish I was dead." She bent down and began to pound her fist against her leg. "No, no, no, no—"

Finally, coming out of his frozen state, James grabbed her wrist before her fist came down again. He lifted her upright and wrapped his arms around her in a tight embrace. "I'm sorry, I'm sorry," he whispered. "I'm so sorry, Elena, for everything that's happened to you." He felt some of the tension begin to leave her body. "I wish I could have been there for you before. I wish I could have prevented this pain that you've suffered. I promise you though, we will set this right. We'll figure it out somehow."

Elena rested her head on his shoulder, still sniffling. Several minutes passed. "So ... you don't hate me?" she whispered. "Despite everything I said, how I lied to you, deceived you, you ... you forgive me?"

James pulled away and gripped her by the biceps. "Elena, what you said, it's difficult to wrap my head around all of it right now, but no, I don't hate you. As incredible as all this is, I believe you, and if what you said is true, then there is nothing to forgive. What happened is not your fault."

"But it *is* my fault. If I didn't get caught up in the darkness in the first place, I—"

"If you didn't, then maybe you never would've met Cole, or maybe you still would have. Maybe you would've lived a happy and peaceful life, or maybe you would've died in a car accident. If you go over all the things you could've done differently, it will drive you crazy. As much as it might suck, things are the way that they are. There's nothing we can do to change that. As screwed up as all of this is, I never would've met you if it wasn't for these dark and dire circumstances that we have found each other in, and for that, I'm not sorry."

Elena leaned in so close that her lips hovered just in front of his. Then she whispered, "Neither am I," before turning and breaking away from his arms. She took off her shoes and socks, rolled up her pants as far as they would go up, and walked into the surf. She stood like that for a while, letting the icy salt water numb her feet. "So now what?" she asked.

"I don't know," James answered after a long pause.

"I've told you everything now. There's nothing more to hide, nothing more to say." She turned to face him. "All that's left is whatever fate has in store for us."

"I don't think we have to leave it up to fate just yet. There has to be something that we can do."

"What? We can't run—even if we got away he would hurt others. We can't just do nothing either. So what, what do we do?"

"We confront him." James said it as if unsure of whether it was a question or a statement.

"Confront him? And do what, have a little chat and be on our merry little way?"

James didn't answer, looking down at the sand.

"If we confront him," Elena said, "there is only one thing we could do. We would have to kill him. I don't know, even after everything he's done to me, I don't know that I could actually kill him. I mean, would you be able to do something like that?"

"He deserves to die. He's evil, so ... yes, I think I could. What other option is there?"

Chapter 11

JAMES AND ELENA: DAY 5, PART 2

"But we don't have to do that tonight, do we?" Elena asked as she sat across the table from James. "I mean, it's already getting late. Cole never gave me a deadline for when I needed to get back to him. I don't think waiting one more night will hurt."

"I suppose you're right." James was fiddling with a pencil, looking at a rough hand-drawn map covered in notes. "Unless you just want to get this over with."

"There's no guarantee that our plan will work. So yes, I would rather put it off for one more day if I can. I would rather spend one more day with you before we plunge back into darkness, maybe for good this time."

"Okay, tomorrow night then." James put the pencil down on the table. "We should probably think about dinner. What would you like?"

Elena looked out the window. "It's a beautiful evening outside." Turning back toward James and with a certain amount of excitement in her voice, she said, "We could make a campfire and cook hot dogs and marshmallows. Do you have any?"

"You know, I think we do." James pulled a package of hot dogs out of the refrigerator and then started rummaging through the pantry. "Ta dah!" he said, holding up a bag of marshmallows. "I couldn't find any hot dog buns, but I think we can manage without them."

"Perfect, I'll start building the fire." A moment later, she was out the door.

James couldn't help but smile at how excited she was about hot dogs and marshmallows. He followed her outside, where she was carrying two pieces of firewood from the stack by the shed down to the shore.

"This will be great, right here," she said, looking at a ring of rocks that was used as a fire pit.

"You'll need some kindling," James said, "or you're never gonna get it started without lighter fluid. Let me see if I can find something in the woods."

So while Elena stacked the wood, James gathered the kindling to start the fire. By the time he returned, she had stacked the wood a good four feet high, and expertly spaced to let the air through. Soon, the flames were large and bright. The sun had set and pure darkness surrounded them except for the firelight illuminating their faces as they sat together on a fallen log.

James handed Elena a stick that he carved into a point at one end along with a hot dog, then took one for himself.

Elena was looking at James as she cooked her hot dog. He was gazing into the fire, concentrating solely on cooking his hot dog to perfection. He looked so— "No!" she squealed as her hot dog slid off the stick and fell into the fire. "Oh, shucks."

"Here, you can have mine," James said.

She laughed. "Yours is burnt to a crisp! I don't want that."

"Hmm, yeah, I like them that way. The trick is to cook it slowly, and only let the skin get all crispy and black after it's been cooking for a while. That way you know that it's done." James took a closer look at his work.

"I'll eat it anyway, thank you." Elena snatched the stick from James's hand and took a bite out of the hot dog. "Ow, oh that's hot. It's actually pretty good though," she added, and then she laughed.

James watched her eat. He enjoyed seeing her happy, but he wasn't able to feel the same way himself. A shadow was still over his mind, and he couldn't shake his feeling of unease. He had been feeling it since Elena's revelation to him earlier that day. Or was it there before that? Yes, he remembered now, it had first surfaced after he had tried to kiss her last night. That look she had for the brief second that she thought he was Cole. The embarrassment and shame and hurt she felt afterward. He wanted to put away that feeling and enjoy this moment with her, but he was unable to do so.

"Well, these hot dogs aren't going to cook themselves. Can I trust you to not waste any more, or do I have to cook them all for you?"

"Stop it," she said, laughing again, and then grabbed another one from the package.

"Wow, I thought you would've liked it black and crispy like your hot dogs," Elena said as she looked at the perfectly golden brown marshmallow that James was holding up.

"No way. If you let it catch fire, the outside turns to ash and the inside is still cold."

"Well, it puts mine to shame."

"Here, you can have this one." James twisted the marshmallow off his stick and handed it to Elena.

"Mmm, it's delicious." She had her eyes closed as she ate it, and when she opened them back up, she saw James staring into the fire. He had a look on his face that troubled her a little. "Maybe I can make you one. I'll try not to burn it."

"Thanks, but I think I'm good." James gave her a slight smile and then continued to look into the fire.

"James, are you thinking about tomorrow?"

"That ... and other things."

"Because I don't want you to worry. Now that we're working together, I know that we can do this. I'm sure of it."

"I'm sorry, I know you don't want to think about that right now."

Elena moved closer to James. "It's fine. We're here in this moment, the two of us together. That's all that matters right now." She leaned in to kiss him. Her lips connected with his, but when he didn't kiss her back, she quickly pulled away. Seeing the expression on his face, she said, "Shit," and then got up and walked away, out into the shadows beyond the fire.

James ran his hands through his hair, and then got up, the log he was sitting on rolling backward as he walked over to her. He saw her silhouette in the moonlight, standing near the water's edge. He stopped a few feet away from her. "It's not that I didn't want to. It's just that, I don't know … I don't know how to explain it." He took an anxious step sideways and put his hand on her shoulder.

Elena shook his hand away and turned to face him. "Don't." She started to walk away, back toward the house, and then she paused and turned around to face him once again. "Look, I don't blame you. Now that you know the truth about me, I get it, things are different now."

"No, it's not that. It's just—"

"All I wanted was to forget for just a little while. To not think about *him*, or tomorrow. To just be in the moment, to experience something beautiful and separate from all of that." And with that, she walked up the path and disappeared into the house.

James stood there for a little while longer, and then made his way back toward the fire, watching the dying flames devour the remaining wood. He stared into the red-hot embers, lost in something deeper or lesser than thought. Then he grabbed the hot dogs and marshmallows and stood up.

He was walking up the stairs, headed for his room. At the landing, he looked down the hall and saw a faint light coming from under Elena's door. He walked over and stopped just outside the door. He was about to say something, or maybe knock, and then he changed his mind, turning to walk back the way he had come.

As Elena lay there in her bed, looking at the ceiling, doubt and confusion filled her mind. Anxiety and fear now replaced all the happiness and optimism that she had felt just a short while earlier. She couldn't stop wondering whether it had all been in her head, the way she thought James felt about her. Then she asked herself whether she really had told James everything, or whether she was still holding something back. Her thoughts drifted back to the last time she had seen Cole, after he had let her out of that room for the last time.

"Don't worry, I'm not going to hurt you," Cole said. "It's obvious that things aren't working out between us. This isn't a prison, it's a home, and I thought that a home is what you wanted. Don't you remember where I found you?"

"Yes, of course I do and I appreciate what you did for me, I really do ..." Elena looked down at the ground. She couldn't stand looking at his face. That pale face with a fake expression of concern plastered on it.

"Where would you be now if I hadn't saved you from that life?" Cole asked. "I had hoped that you would come around, that you would see what you had here, but it seems clear now that our ways must part. You are free to leave."

Elena looked up at him suddenly with a hesitant look of hope in her eyes.

"But there's still the matter of the debt that you still owe me. Everything I did for you wasn't free."

The hope in her eyes disappeared. "But I don't have any money. I could pay you back when I get—"

"I don't want your money." The expression on Cole's face changed, abruptly growing more menacing, more animated—excited. He started to pace around her. "No, I have a better idea. The way I see it is that I saved your life, and therefore you owe me your life. If you still want to leave like the ungrateful bitch that you apparently are, then I still need a payment worthy of that debt." He stopped pacing and looked her in the eyes. "There is a man that recently took up residence at a house on the coast, not far from here. I need you to go down there and get him to come up here to me. He also has to come up here voluntarily and of his own free will—this is very important. How you do that is up to you, but I imagine it shouldn't be too difficult a task for someone like you to manage. Once you do this, you are free to go."

"And what are you going to do to him after I get him up here?"

"What do you think?" he yelled. Then he softened his voice. "Why do you care? You've only ever cared about yourself. He's just some lowlife trash, anyway. A life for a life, that's how it has to be. The debt must be paid. If you don't deliver him, if you try to run from it, if you go to the police, or even if you just honestly fail, I will kill you. I will hunt you down and find you, only now it won't be just you that has to die, others will die as well. Maybe it will be a friend or a relative, or maybe it will be several random strangers. I can send you pictures of their lifeless bodies so that you will know the suffering that you have caused before I finally come for you in the end. But I know that you'll do the right thing."

Cole grabbed Elena's face by her chin and cheeks, contorting her features, and stuffed a folded piece of paper into her pocket. "This isn't the way it had to be. It could've been different, but because of your own selfishness his fate will be on your hands, not mine. This is *your* debt, the consequences of *your* actions that you will now have to live with. Now get out of here!" He pushed her away by her face.

Elena stumbled back into a chair, knocking it over. Regaining her balance, she took one look back at Cole and then ran for the door. She was in a state of panic and fright as she fumbled with the doorknob. Then she ran for the woods. She found herself running downhill along a narrow trail and thinking of nothing other than getting as far away from that awful house as she could. Eventually, she tripped over a root and fell to the ground. Exhausted and out of breath, she lay on the ground for several minutes.

Elena crawled over to a tree and rested her back against it. Her mind was racing. *What a mess you have gotten yourself into now, Elena. I have no water, no food. There's no way I'm gonna go back up there, though. Where am I, and where am I even supposed to find this man, anyway?* Then she remembered the paper that Cole shoved in her pocket. She pulled it out and unfolded it, seeing that it was a map. There was a simplistic drawing of a house with the word HOME written below it. *This must be where I came from, although "home" would be the last way I'd describe it.* There were two lines drawn leading away from the house. One in bold black marker, and one in pen that was also highlighted in red. She tried to remember what she saw when she ran from the house, but her mind was a fog.

Wait, the bay was out to her right, she remembered it clearly now. That meant that she had to be on the highlighted red path. The path led down to a road, and with her finger she followed the red highlight as it went partway along the road and broke off onto another path. It ended at a small sketch of a house with the word TARGET written below it. She put the map away and continued walking down the hill.

At the bottom of the hill, Elena found the road and followed it. When she reached the end of the red path on the map, she staked out a position in the trees with a good vantage point of a beautiful log house. It had a much more homey and welcoming look than the house she had just come from. A man was standing at the edge of the shore, staring off across the bay. *That has to be him.* She watched him as he walked back into the house. Then she slipped back deeper into the woods. When she approached a clearing at the edge of a stream, she stopped.

"What am I doing here?" she asked herself. "This is horrible, it's too fucking terrible." Elena dropped to her knees. *Fuck, how did it come to this? I know I've made poor decisions, did horrible things. If it was just his life or mine, it would be easier. I could end it all right now, and that would be the end of it. No. No, you can do this. You've always done what you had to do to survive. But this is different. I never had to kill anyone before, and that's what I would be doing here, even if it isn't with my own hands. But Cole did say that he was worthless trash, that he didn't even deserve to live. Maybe it wouldn't be so bad for him to take my place. But who am I to make that decision? Why couldn't he have just killed me instead of putting me in this impossible predicament, where every option is just too horrible? I don't want to die, I really don't, but do I deserve to live?*

Elena forced herself to stop thinking and tried to clear her mind. She sat and listened to the water flow by her. Finally, she decided to get up and walk back to the edge of the woods to see if she could get another look at the man.

When Elena looked out toward the house, the man was standing on the front porch and looking out over the bay again. He disappeared into the house, then came out the back and started for the woods. She decided to follow him discreetly, not knowing what she would or should do. The man hiked through the woods, and Elena followed as he walked up a hill and finally stopped at the edge of a cliff. She didn't have a good view of him from her position, so she made her way around him through the trees, trying to be as quiet as she could. She came out to the edge of the cliff maybe twenty yards from where the man was standing. Even from that distance, she thought she could make out the expression on his face.

What is he doing? Then she could see him slowly leaning forward. *Oh shit, I've seen that look before, I've even felt it myself. If he kills himself, what am I supposed to tell Cole? I doubt that he'll accept his suicide as proper payment, and who knows what he'll do then. Maybe ... no, that's crazy, but what other option is there? I have to. He'll save me. If he doesn't, maybe that's better anyway, and all of this will be over then. There's no more time to think, I have to act. Fuck.*

And then she leapt.

Elena came back to the present, lying in her bed, staring at the ceiling. *And here I am now, as confused as ever about how I feel about him, and about how he feels about me. And if we can kill Cole, then what? Happiness ... a happy ending. Me and James happily ever after? Somehow that doesn't feel real, especially with the way he was tonight. I can't think about all that right now or it will drive me crazy.* And with that thought, Elena slowly drifted off into an uneasy sleep.

Elena found herself in total darkness, and couldn't see anything. She spun around a few times, trying to figure out where she was, but couldn't see a thing. She waved her hand in front of her face—still nothing. The fear was growing inside of her, the fear of unknowing, of being alone, the fear of the darkness so thick around her, almost suffocating her. As the fear turned into panic, she thought she saw something. Yes, she was certain of it, a light, she saw some kind of light—there it was again. At first it was just a flicker, and then it grew constant. Elena walked toward it, feeling the wet grass on her bare feet as she moved toward the light that was growing brighter in the blackness that surrounded her. Her feet, why was she barefoot? Why didn't she have shoes on? Where was she? She couldn't remember how she had gotten here. As she got closer to the light—which didn't really look like a flame, but also didn't seem artificial somehow—the light suddenly began to fade, and then went out completely.

"NO!" she shouted. "No, don't leave me, I don't even know where I am. Light, come back to me!" She started to cry. Suddenly, she felt arms wrap around her.

"Shhh, don't cry," came a voice next to her ear. "I am here. I will never leave you."

"James," she said, relieved. "I'm so happy you're here—" She turned around, but James was some distance away from her. And the look on his face was one of such great anguish, a despair unlike anything Elena had ever seen on his face. She could see him clearly, even in the darkness. She ran toward him, half yelling, half weeping. "James, what's wrong? What is it ... James stop it, what's happening!" James started to fade away, as if he was fading away into nothingness, until he was completely gone.

Then Elena was alone again in complete darkness. The panic that she felt earlier had grown into hysteria. Her shirt was wet, the cold fabric clinging to her stomach. *Why would it be wet? I haven't been in the water recently, have I?* She could start to see her hand that she held out in front of her. There was a light that started to illuminate the darkness again, and looking at her hand, she could now see that it was red. *Is that ... blood?* Then she turned around to see where the light was coming from. There was a fire—or maybe just a flame, or maybe it wasn't a flame, she wasn't sure. In front of the fire, or flame, or whatever it was, there appeared a shape of a man. *James, is that you?* No, it wasn't James; it was Cole. She could see his hideous, vicious smile. He was moving toward her, faster and faster, until he was right in front of her. Elena threw herself down onto the wet grass, unable to face him. "NO, NO!" she shouted. "No, this can't be real! Get away from me, get away from me! What is happening, this can't be real, don't let this be real!"

"No, no, get away from me!" Elena was still yelling. When she opened her eyes, she saw the familiar shadows of her room, and felt the bed that she was lying in. She touched her face and felt the wetness of tears on her cheeks. She couldn't shake the fear that was still as present as it had been while she was dreaming. Looking at her clock, she saw that it read 2:13 A.M. She got out of bed and started to pace. She had a sudden urge to go down the hall and knock on James's door, to find comfort in his presence and in his embrace, and in his calm and reassuring words. But James had pulled away from her, had rejected her. Not that she blamed him. Now that he knew the truth about her, why wouldn't he reject her?

The fear had subsided to a dull yet constant pitch in her head. She turned on the overhead light, lay back down on the bed, and stared up at the ceiling, focusing on the wavy lines of plaster. After a while, an uneasy and troubled sleep finally crept up on her again as fragments of her previous nightmare wove in and out of new dreamscapes.

Chapter 12

GEORGE AND ANNA: ONE MONTH EARLIER

Anna woke up, seeing daylight shining through the curtains. She must have slept the entire night. Yet somehow she felt more tired now than when she went to bed. Looking over, she saw that George was gone. Probably outside as he often was with the rising sun. Despite what had happened, they were as distant as ever. Not that Anna cared much. In fact, she seemed to care about very little lately. Oftentimes she didn't know what she was doing any more. Just letting the days pass by and that was about it. Sometimes when she woke up the thought would come to her, as she was thinking on this morning, that this wasn't any kind of life at all.

She reached over and opened the nightstand drawer. She pulled out a framed photograph and looked at the smiling couple. *Who are these people? She was me once, but I don't remember her. That woman was happy. She loved her man, her life. That woman has long been dead.* She took the picture out of the frame and grabbed a sharpie from the drawer. With it she wrote SHE IS DEAD over the woman in the photograph. Anna put it back in the frame and looked at it once more. Then she suddenly threw it against the wall. She got up from the bed and made her way over to where it lay on the floor. The glass was cracked, making the faces behind it look fractured. She shoved the picture underneath the bed with her foot.

She walked into the bathroom, not bothering to look at herself in the mirror—she already knew what she would look like and didn't care. She opened the medicine cabinet and grabbed a bottle of prescription pills. Maybe George was right. Maybe things were better now. Although if this was better, then she couldn't remember how bad it was before. It was true that she didn't really have the dreams any more. Or the dreams were still there, but they were now all hazy and distant, like looking at something from a great distance through glasses that were much too strong for your eyes. Perhaps this was better. But she couldn't help feeling that there was something that she was supposed to see, something important that she was missing, some action she was supposed to take.

The drugs may have taken the dreams away, but they dulled and blurred the waking world as well. She felt numb, disconnected from the world and everything in it. She looked at the bottle before putting it back—

Truosetine, some new kind of antidepressant. The idea of being hopped up on prescription drugs was something she had always hated, especially something like antidepressants. But she had made a promise to George, and after he had convinced the doctor not to commit her—thank God for that—she thought she owed him this much at least.

She chuckled slightly as she recalled what the doctor had asked her—the same question the first doctor had asked.

"And when did you first start having these kind of dreams," Dr. Phillips murmured.

Everyone seemed to think that she must have suffered some traumatic event that triggered these dreams. But they didn't suddenly happen. They weren't absent one day and there the next. No, they came on slowly, gradually, years after she married George, and each one was slightly more visceral than the one before. And slowly she started to question whether there was something more to them, that they were more than mere dreams.

And it wasn't only the dreams. Even when she was awake, there would be times when someone would pass by and it seemed like she could hear their thoughts. Words bouncing through her head that she knew were not her own. Sometimes it would be just feelings, emotion, hate, desire—she could feel them radiating off other people. She never had any control over it. Sometimes it would happen, other times it wouldn't. So, though Anchorage wasn't that big of a city compared to the metropolises in the lower forty-eight, it still became much too large to tolerate once she started having these experiences. The only blessing was that she had never experienced George's thoughts, although there were times when she wished she could hear what he was thinking.

Here and there she would see the goodness and kindness in people's hearts, and it would warm her to know it. More often, though, she would see the selfishness and hate that people harbored within themselves. And a few times she experienced the feelings of the truly despicable.

There was one time when she was walking in Kincaid Park and she saw a man sitting on a bench. The look on his face troubled her. He was watching a woman jog past him when it hit her. She felt his lust, then she saw his fantasy unfold. Raping her, his hands around her neck, watching the life go out of her eyes. But that wasn't what scared her the most. What truly frightened her was the sensation that not only had he fantasized about this before, he had actually done it. She drank more than half a bottle of scotch when she got home, trying to burn away those feelings and images.

In dreams, though, it was different, even worse than when she was awake. In dreams she could see into other people's lives, and it usually wasn't the good parts.

Anna still did not know why she started having these experiences, or even if there was a reason. Maybe the ability had always been lying dormant inside her. Sometimes she thought it was a gift, laid upon her to give her the ability to make a real difference in this world. Perhaps she suffered because she hadn't found a way to use what she saw to actually help people.

An hour later Anna was walking in the forest, gazing up at the Sitka spruce dripping water from the melting snow. She hadn't seen George. He was probably hunting, although she knew that was mainly just an excuse to get away from her. He hardly ever came back with a kill.

As she hiked, something seemed to seep through the drug-enforced barrier in her mind. She took a deep breath, breathing in the fresh, clean air. There was always something about being outside, surrounded by nothing but nature and beauty, that allowed her to cut through the fog and haze in her mind, at least for a little while. It was March, and spring would come soon. Not more than ten feet in front of her, a ptarmigan, almost invisible in its winter plumage, scraped at the snow for food underneath. She took a few steps forward, hoping to get a better look, then she slipped on a patch of ice and went tumbling down the hill. She sat up, collecting her bearings and making sure she wasn't seriously hurt, when she jumped to her feet, startled by a nearby voice.

"I'm so sorry, I didn't mean to scare you. I was just checking to see if you were okay."

Anna looked to her left and saw a man walking toward her. It was none other than Cole Bontone. "That's okay, thank you," she said. "I'm fine."

"It's been a while, hasn't it?" Cole asked.

"Yes. It's Cole, right?"

"Yes, that's right. And you are Anna, Anna Green. I could never forget you, however brief our meeting."

A coldness seeped into Anna's bones. Her mind suddenly became very clear and sharp. He was smiling, a very kind, warm smile. Of course, Anna saw right through it. She knew who—what—he was. It occurred to her that he might also see who she was, and what she could see in him. It was in this moment that his face suddenly changed. It was still his face, but yet somehow not the same. The eyes were maniacal, so wide and alive with a look of pleasure combined with hate. Anna shuddered and quickly turned away, unable to bear those piercing eyes. Eyes that seemed to look within her, trying to penetrate the depths of her soul.

When she finally looked back, it was just the normal kindly face again. She was almost ready to dismiss what she had seen as nothing more than some freak moment of delusion. But she knew better. Her past experience had taught her that. She had dismissed these visions and feelings and dreams that she'd had about people before, and she had seen the consequences of her inaction. A great unease came over her, and he could sense it.

"Are you all right?" Cole asked. "You seem pale."

"Yes, I'm fine. It's just the cold."

"I would love to have both you and George up to my place for dinner sometime, if it's not too much of a trouble."

Without knowing where it came from, Anna suddenly spoke with a very matter of fact and stern voice. "I know who you are."

Something changed in both Cole's face and his tone of voice as he answered her. Like he had expected her to say something like that all along. "And I know you, Anna Green. We will meet again, I'm sure of it." He turned and started walking away. "And soon, oh yes, very soon. I'm quite looking forward to it."

As Anna watched him leave, she felt the fear again. The kind of fear that she hadn't felt since she started taking those pills. But this time, the fear didn't make her cower. It didn't make her want to hide until it went away. This time she held onto it—it was better than the fog and dullness of mind that the drugs created. She climbed on top of it like a wave, used it to motivate her, to fuel her, to propel her forward. Because as she was walking back down toward the house, she knew what she had to do. Was she scared? Sure, but she wasn't going to let the fear defeat her any longer. She finally had seen what her purpose was, and that her life could have meaning yet. She had finally seen what she had to do, even if it was the last thing that she would ever do.

When she got back to the house, the first thing she did was go upstairs and flush all the pills down the toilet and throw the bottle in the garbage.

That night, she dreamed again, a dream that felt very visceral and real. She dreamed of a large house, a house she had dreamed of before, only now she could see more. She could see the entire area around it. It was up on a tree-lined hill, with a clearing on top to give a breathtaking view of the bay down below, and the side of the mountain behind it climbing yet higher. She went inside the house and she could see *him*, she could see Cole. The face she saw on him was the face that she had only seen in that one brief moment, his true face.

When she woke up that morning, she wasn't afraid. She wasn't afraid of anything any more, not Cole, not death. Her inaction to change the circumstances surrounding her haunted her no longer. She thought of what she had seen in her dream, the path up to that house.

Chapter 13

JAMES AND ELENA: DAY 6

After Elena finished taking a shower, the dreams from the previous night already felt vague and distant. As she dressed, she thought she saw something poking out between the mattress and the box spring of the bed, which had been exposed when she tore the sheets partially off during her nightmare. She pulled out a thin notebook with a black cover. There was a note written in red marker: *George, Read This and Find Some Kind of Peace. Your Ever-Loving Wife, Anna.*

When Elena finished reading it, she lay back on the bed, setting the notebook down next to her. *I've been here with James for what, five, six days? Yes, this would be the sixth. George and Anna were gone before James found the place, which I think he said was about ten days before I found him. Let's see ... I would've been with Cole during that time. That would mean that when Anna wrote this—and assuming that she acted upon what she wrote—it must have happened before I ever met Cole. So Anna didn't go through with it ... or she failed.*

She got up and rushed downstairs. "James, you have to see what I found." But he wasn't there. Then she looked out the window and saw him, his back to her as he sat on a large rock close to the water's edge, staring out into the horizon. The sky was overcast, and a slight breeze gently rippled his grey hoodie. Elena set the notebook on the table and put on her shoes.

"Hey there, you won't believe what I found," she said as she approached him. He didn't respond, so Elena walked around the rock to face him. His expression was distant, as if deep in thought. Without saying another word, she silently sat down next to him on the rock and looked out into the distance as well.

A few minutes later, a light rain started to fall. Neither of them moved. Then James said, "It seems appropriate somehow, it seems right ... the rain. It's beautiful, don't you think? At a time like this, it's better than the sun."

"I suppose so," Elena said.

"I loved driving. There's something about just being on the open road, listening to music and watching the scenery go by. The freedom of it, the expectations of not knowing what to expect. I didn't mind being alone—sure, it would get lonely after a while, but for me I think it was actually better than having someone else there talking nonstop for ten hours a day. The Great Plains flew by me, the vast openness of the Dakotas ..." James trailed off and became lost in his thoughts again.

"That was when you left, right?"

"It was about a month ago," James said. "Yes, it was the beginning of April. But there really isn't much to say about all of that."

"Perhaps, but I'd still like to hear it anyway," Elena said. "And after everything I've told you about myself, well, it would be nice to hear someone else's story. Even if you think it's small and uninteresting, it's still a part of you, and I want to hear it."

"But I've never had any big trauma in my life. No insurmountable tragedy to come to terms with. My life was never what you might categorize as bad, or rough, or especially difficult. I had a good childhood, a good life. Of course, things were never perfect, but I had it better than most do nowadays."

"So why were you on that cliff? Something had to drive you to that kind of moment?"

"First of all, I don't know if I actually would have jumped. But when you look at all the people that have done it, if you were to see why they actually did it, I think you would see that it's for so many different reasons, and some of them might not seem so substantial. I think that often it's not much more than an utter sense of hopelessness, and a lack of purpose. A way to escape the suffering of this life, and the hope that something better awaits them on the other side."

James stood up, still looking out into the distance. "When I left, I guess I was just trying to find out if there was something more out there, in another place. That, and to try and experience life more—whatever that even means. I felt that I had done almost nothing with my life, nothing good, nothing bad. I wanted to feel alive again, really alive, not just going through your daily routine and job day after day, hardly feeling anything at all.

"I wanted to see the Pacific Ocean first, before heading up through Canada. And after I crossed the mountains in Washington, I finally saw it, the coast, the ocean. It was wild, and there was a chilling breeze with rain pelting against my jacket. The waves were ferocious, tall, cresting, and seething with foam and crashing water, before collapsing in and upon itself in a sea of white froth. Large rocks like islands sticking out high above the water. Waves crashing upon rock in a spectacular spray of water and foam. The sea, wild, ferocious and untamable. I loved it, it was something pure, unspoiled by man or anything else. Then I drove up through Canada, enjoying long days of driving through vast mountain ranges that never seemed to end. By the time I crossed the border into Alaska, none of it had yet bored me. But after I had been in Anchorage for a few days, in a city filled with people, loneliness and some form of feeling you could probably call depression really started setting in. Before then I had a destination, a place where I was headed for, but beyond that destination I didn't really have any kind of plan. I went to a few bars, but could never really enjoy my time there. Too loud, and too many people that I had nothing to say to."

James started to pace. "One evening I found something that I truly enjoyed. I started hiking out along the coast to a spot where there weren't any people, with a bottle of wine and a cigar, and then I'd put on some music. There's this wonderful and beautiful moment, when you have that perfect buzz from the alcohol, and you're listening to some of the most beautiful music that you've ever heard. There isn't a person around, and sometimes there's eagle's flying overhead, or there are sea lions, or seals lying on the rocks at low tide. The beauty of nature surrounds you, and you start dancing, dancing like nobody can see you, because no one can. In that moment, it's a truly great and beautiful moment to find yourself in. Often though, as I was walking back to my car, sadness would set in again, as quick as the happiness and beautiful moment I'd experienced just a short while before had come. I'd think of all my regrets, my missed opportunities, and how I still hadn't done anything of true worth yet in my life. I'd drift in and out between happiness and sadness, sadness taking up the vast majority of my life. But I still manage to find beauty in the sadness that I so often find myself in. I try to be thankful for everything that God has blessed me with. I try to get my mind right, to focus on what truly matters, to try and do what is good and right, looking for something beyond myself. But I often have no idea how to go about that, or how to even go looking for something like that. I feel like there's something that is missing in me, or broken. That part of a person that makes them able to connect with other people. Because when I spend too much time alone I'm melancholy, and when I'm around people I feel out of place.

"That's when I happened to find this house, out in the middle of nowhere, out of place. At first I really enjoyed being here, but then some kind of darkness started to grab hold of my mind. My thoughts turned dark, and that's when you found me up at that cliff."

James stopped pacing and stood facing Elena. "See, I told you there wasn't much to say. I don't know why that was apparently enough to send me to a cliff. It sounds even more pathetic when I say it out loud." Tears were shining in his eyes. "Why, Elena? Why am I like this? Why do I always feel like I can never be a part of this world? Why do I always feel sad when it seems like I have no reason to? Why have I met you, when God knows I haven't ever deserved to find anyone as remarkable as you? And that someone like you would ever have any interest in someone like me?"

"James, I wish I could tell you, but I don't know why we are the way we are. I don't know if we truly have the ability to change ourselves, or if our fate is already set in stone. And why would you even want to be part of this world? This world is dark and cruel, superficial and fake. Isn't it better to be apart from it?"

Elena stood up and rested her forehead against his while holding onto his shoulders. "Listen to me, James. It doesn't matter if you think that what you felt is small or insignificant. It's real, just as real as my own feelings. You hang onto that; you hang onto it because it's all that you have. You own it, because it is you. Without it, what would you be? What would any of us be? Your past experiences and feelings are what make you who you are. Whether it's good or bad, you accept it and move on. The past is what makes us who we are, the present is who we have become. Don't you see? We have come down different paths, gone through sorrow, despair, and loneliness that were each our own. But now we are together, somehow we met each other, and somehow we are right for each other. I don't know how or why, but right now maybe that's all that matters, that we are together."

James pulled away from her, taking several steps back and then turning away.

"What's wrong? James …"

"You still don't understand, do you?"

"What?"

"I found something, a realization," James said. "There was a moment, while I was drifting along the Kenai

Peninsula before I got here. I discovered something about myself. I accepted what I had already known for some time but just refused to acknowledge, to accept. I am only who I am, and nothing more. There isn't any use in trying to change who I am because I would never be able to. I accepted that I would never be able to fit in with the rest of the world in the way most people do, and that I'm alone. It's not that I want to be alone, or even choose to be, it's just that I am. I'm not good with other people. When everything is said and done, I go through this life alone. And even though there is a lot of loneliness and sadness that comes with that kind of life, there's also a real beauty and peace to be found there as well. You see, all of us are different. We can choose what we do with our lives, but we can't choose what our nature is, loud or quiet, aggressive or meek, intellectual or down to earth, these things we can't really control."

"Maybe you're right. There are things that we can't change, but there are some things we can. I'm not sure what you're getting at, though. Are you talking about us? Just because you've spent most of your life alone doesn't mean it always has to be like that."

"But don't you see? It *is* like that. We've been dancing around this subject the whole time, about whether there's something more here between us or not. Although I would like for it to be different, the way I see it is that it can never work out for us. To put it bluntly, I'm broken, and you're fucked up."

"What?" Elena said, slightly shocked. "How could you say that? How could you say that about me? You know what I've been through."

"I'm sorry. I'm just trying to say that maybe that's why you're trying so hard for things to work out between us. Despite how much both of us may want this, in the end … I don't know, I don't think we're right. You don't deserve to have me tied around your neck, dragging you down."

"Well, maybe that's not for you to decide. And if being alone is so great, then why were you on that cliff?"

"I never said it was so great. Of course it's not, nothing really is, though. I mean look at where we are, look at all the surrounding beauty. I always thought I would be happy in a place like this, with the solitude and beauty of it all. And for a little while, I was. But then something changes, the place turns on you, and like a switch turning off a light, everything about this place seems meaningless. And if a place like this can turn dark and horrid, where can you go to escape from it? What can you do to change it? It's like you have this clarity. You know you have options, you know you could do this or that, go here or there. But you also know—and you know it with such a surety—that it doesn't matter what you do. It won't change anything, it won't change who you are or how you feel. When you entered my life, I thought that maybe things could be different, but I understand now that they aren't. In the end, what really matters? What is there to truly live for?"

Elena threw up her hands. "What is there to live for? How about life itself? And that even if it's not so great, you still keep on living it, because that's what you do. You find some kind of reason, or a hope that things will get better someday. And even if they don't, maybe you get one moment, one moment that's so beautiful that it makes going through everything that's terrible in this life worth it. It's not supposed to be up to us when we leave this world. Whether you call it God, or fate, or something else, we carry on in this world until we can't any longer, because that is how it is."

"Yes, that's how it is. But is there any more than that?" James asked as he started to walk back to the house.

Elena watched him walk up the path and close the door without looking back. "Yes," she said. "There has to be."

As Elena finished the sandwich she was eating for lunch, sitting at the table with James, she couldn't help feeling like they were still strangers, despite everything that they had shared together. They were back at square one, although Elena had no idea why. The feelings she had for him, feelings that seemed real and had been growing stronger; they meant nothing now? She hated this silence between them, this tension.

"I can't take this any more," she said, abruptly getting up from her chair. She grabbed a bottle of whisky and stuffed it in a backpack and went for the door. "If you want to be alone, fine." Then she slammed the door behind her.

"Elena," James said. But it was too late. She was already gone. He watched her from the window, unsure of what to do as she walked along the shore. Instead of continuing to walk until she was far out of sight, like James had expected her to do, she dropped the backpack to the ground and then took a swig from a bottle before sitting down herself. *What the hell am I doing?* James thought as he made his way toward the door. As he hurried down the path, she took the elastic band out of her hair, letting it blow loose in the breeze. Before he could say anything, she handed him the bottle of whiskey.

"Look, this is our last day before ... before tonight," she said. "I can't think of anything better to do than get drunk on the beach with you. Oh—" Elena dug into her backpack and pulled out a portable speaker that she synced to her phone, and then played music. Deep, sad, and beautiful music.

James took a swig from the bottle, eyeing Elena as he did.

"Come on, James, forget about everything else for a little while. Just be in this moment, be here with me."

"That sounds like a good idea." James handed the bottle back to Elena.

They sat on a rock side by side, looking out across the water, listening to music and drinking. After a few more pulls from the bottle, Elena got up and started to dance a little as she softly sang along to some of the lyrics. James joined her, letting the music move him along with the buzz he was starting to get from the whisky. Soon, neither of them cared what they looked like and just let the alcohol and music take over. In that moment, they didn't worry about what might happen that night. They danced separately yet together, like they had on that prior night before in front of the fireplace. They just enjoyed that moment, as both of them knew it wouldn't last long.

The space between their bodies closed. Then James leaned over and kissed Elena, several light soft kisses. He paused, pulling away slightly to look at her, and then leaned in again. This time, he kissed her with more passion, feeling the weight of her lips against his own. He started to explore her mouth more, wanting to take in as much of her as he could. Their bodies locked together on the shore as the music continued to play.

Elena stumbled on a rock, and she fell to the sand, pulling James down with her. As he lay there next to her, he took a moment to let his eyes move over her body before they rested on her face. He moved partially on top of her and kissed her neck, then her lips again as his free hand roamed across her body. When he found her breast, he let his hand linger there as he continued to kiss her. An almost frantic energy built in Elena as she kissed him with a growing urgency. She took his arm and pressed his hand against the place between her legs.

James pulled away from her and sat up in the sand. They looked at each other for a moment before James said, "I can't do this." Then he got up and started to walk down the shoreline.

Elena sat up and watched him go. He stopped some ways away and looked across the bay. Then he pulled out a cigar and lit it. She got up and walked over to the bottle of whiskey lying in the sand, and took a long swig from it. She watched as James continued to walk again, moving farther away. "I guess it's just you and me now," she said, looking at the bottle she was holding. She sat on a rock and stared out at the horizon. One small tear escaped from her eye and rolled down her cheek. She didn't bother wiping it away.

The music continued to play.

Chapter 14

GEORGE AND ANNA: ONE MONTH EARLIER

Anna paced the room. She knew what she had to do, but didn't know how to deal with George. She knew that she couldn't tell him. He would try to stop her, he never would be able to understand. Yet she felt she needed to leave some kind of explanation behind. She owed him that, at least.

When she finished writing, she found a red marker. After a moment of thought she wrote, *George, Read This and Find Some Kind of Peace.* And then below that, in smaller print, *Your Ever-Loving Wife, Anna.*

Anna set the notebook on a pillow on the bed, knowing that George wouldn't be up here for at least a couple of hours. She walked downstairs, put on her boots and jacket, and went outside. She looked over the bay and then back at the house. In that moment, she desperately wished that things could be different. But they were the way they were, and she knew that this was the way they had to end.

Anna walked into the backyard, then past their little garage, as she decided not to take the car. She turned and walked down the road for about a mile until she reached the trail that she had seen in her dream, the trail that led to his house. She climbed the hill until she saw it. Yes, this was it. This was Cole's house. Her dreams had shown her the way, just as she'd known they would.

George punched the tree in front of him, and then a second time. "Fuck!" he yelled as his fist connected again. The tree remained virtually unmarked, save for a small amount of blood left by his knuckles. Could he have been so wrong? Could he have been wrong about everything?

He thought about when he had gone up to Cole's house on the hill the other day. It was the first time he had been up there, the only time. They were sitting on the edge of a bluff overlooking the bay, smoking cigars.

"Like smoke, vapors and shadows in the night," Cole said. "Illusions and delusions. Delirium in the darkness of the mind."

George didn't know what he was talking about. But there was something in the way that Cole was saying it that unsettled him.

"Do you know what is reality?" Cole said. "Can you differentiate between the physical and the metaphysical? Tell me George, do you know yourself? Your wife? Do you know what she dreams about in the dark, when all light is gone and the physical world starts to melt away? You better keep an eye on that one, Georgie. There is something ... something in her. Something in her that you don't understand, can't understand. I saw it the first time I saw her. So tell me, do you know your wife? I mean really know her?"

George watched as Cole blew out a cloud of smoke as he finished his last sentence. There was something in his eyes, some glint he had never noticed before. He repressed the urge to shudder. A thought suddenly sprang into his mind, a thought that almost didn't feel like his own.

She was right; she was right about him.

George was looking at his bloody knuckles as his mind came back to the present. By the time he had come home that day, he had mostly dismissed that thought, but now it had come back. Was Anna right about him? Was she right about everything all along? He had never believed her. He just couldn't. He wasn't able to wrap his mind around how such a thing could be possible.

George could sense that something was about to happen. Something was wrong—something had been wrong for some time now, of course, but now he felt like it was about to be too late. He had to do something. He had to stop Anna from doing whatever she was about to do.

George quickly made his way back to the house. He called her name as he entered through the door, hoping she was still here. When he walked into their bedroom he stopped short when he saw something on the bed. Lying on a pillow was a small black notebook with red writing on the cover. He read the message and opened it to the first page.

George, you believed things would be better, we both believed. We believed that moving out here would fix all of our problems. It was a beautiful dream, and for a little while at least that dream was a reality. But I realize now, more than I ever have before, that people never change. I am who I am, and I can't keep running away from that anymore. I know what I have to do. There is something meaningful that I can do here, where I can yet serve a purpose. I don't expect you to understand at first, and it's why I couldn't tell you in person, but I hope you will find a way to be at peace with it, as I have.

If you think you might have failed me, know that you haven't. I want you to know that you have been the best thing in my life, and that you would move us all the way out here to try and fix me means so much to me. But I can find no peace in this world, no rest for my mind. As you read this, it will be too late to do anything. It's already over.

Your ever-loving wife and friend, Anna.

"No, what have you done?" George said. He dropped the notebook like it was burning his hands. After staring at it for a moment, he picked it up and shoved it between the mattress and the box spring. He ran down the stairs and then out of the house, but stopped after going only a few yards. *It might not be too late. I still might be able to help her. But where is she?* He turned in a circle, pulling on his hair. There was something taped to the door. He pulled the note off and opened it.

Do you know yourself?
Do you know your wife?
Do you know where she is?
If you do, you better hurry.
Your friend, Cole Bontone

"Motherfucker," George said as he crumpled up the note.

Chapter 15

JAMES AND ELENA: DAY 6, PART 2

"Pull over here," Elena said. The sun had set, and they were driving down the gravel road only a mile from the house. "We'll have to walk the rest of the way. It's just up that hill."

"Is this really the only path up to his place?" James asked.

"I know he has a car. I think there's some kind of driveway that goes down toward another area of the mountain, but this is the way I came, and I'm not sure how to go around the other way. Besides, this way is probably more discreet."

James reached underneath his seat and pulled out a handgun. It was a 9mm Glock 19 that he had found at the house. He handed it to Elena. "Have you ever shot one before? There's no safety, but—"

Elena gave him a look as if to say, *are you serious?* "Please," she said, grabbing the gun. She dropped the magazine, looking at it to make sure it was fully loaded before slamming it back in. "I think I can handle it."

"Okay then," James said as he grabbed another handgun from under his seat. His very own Sig Sauer P220 .45 that he had taken with him from Illinois and smuggled over the Canadian border. He got out of the car and put the gun into the holster on the side of his belt. "You ready?"

Elena handed him a flashlight. "Will I ever be?"

James gave her a sympathetic look but didn't say anything. And with that, they headed up the hill along the trail into the woods.

There was still a little light out, but underneath all the trees it was already quite dark, and they turned the flashlights on. After they had been walking for maybe half an hour and James was about to take a rest, worn out by the mostly steady incline of the hill, he saw where another trail branched off to the left of the one they were on. "Left?" James shined his flashlight back toward Elena, and she nodded her head.

He had barely started to walk down this new trail when he came across a rope blocking the path. Shining his light about—it was now quite dark—he saw a sign on either side of the rope reading PRIVATE PROPERTY, NO TRESPASSING. He ducked under the rope and continued walking. Just up ahead, there were several more signs nailed to trees. One read DO NOT ENTER, another TRESPASSERS WILL BE SHOT, and a few more reiterated NO TRESPASSING and PRIVATE PROPERTY.

James realized that Elena was no longer right behind him. He looked back and saw her standing motionless on the path a little farther down. As he walked back toward her, shining his flashlight in her direction, he saw the look of worry on her face. "What's wrong?" he asked.

"I had a feeling just now," Elena said.

"What kind of feeling?"

"Like ... we won't be coming back down."

James was now close enough to see the expression on her face in the natural light of the stars and moon shining through the trees. "Hey, come on now. That's just the fear talking. We'll make it through this, you'll see."

"But you don't know him like I do, James. He's sick in the head, he finds joy in other people's suffering, but he's not stupid either."

"I know, but you said it yourself that this is our best shot. We have to be rid of him, and this is the only way."

"I don't know. Sometimes I think it's impossible to escape this darkness. Even if we kill Cole, will we ever truly be free of him, or will his shadow still always follow us? No matter what I do, darkness always keeps its grip on me." There was a long pause before she continued. "I hate this, James. What's happened to us, I feel like we really had something together, but now there's only distance, so much space separating us. I don't want it to end like this, not when we're about to face something that we might not come back from." Elena rested her head against James's shoulder. "I wish ... I wish we made love when we were on the beach."

James looked at her, but he was unable to find the words to reply.

Elena's eyes were watery and her voice cracked as she asked, "Why did you walk away? Why? I know you wanted it too ... I know you did. But then you just left. Since then, we haven't even had a genuine conversation. I just wanted to experience something beautiful and wonderful, something to hang on to when we have to face *this*—" She pointed up the hill. "Whatever awaits us up there. I wanted to feel something that wasn't *him*, that wasn't Cole's touch, but yours. I wanted to feel what it was like to be loved again." Tears came into her eyes as she continued, "I wanted to feel what it would be like to make love to you. Are you going to just stand there and tell me that you didn't want that too?"

"No."

"But you pushed me away, just walked away—why? If this is the end, I don't want it to end like this. So tell me, James, why did you walk away? If we die tonight, won't you wish that we had truly made the most of our time together?"

Why did you walk away? It was a question James kept asking himself. He had wanted more than anything to keep going, to ravish her, to take her in, to be with her completely. There was never a thing that he had wanted more. But there was something that made him stop, that kept him from doing what he so wanted to do. He wasn't sure what it was, but in that moment he felt that if he continued, he would be putting everything that might yet happen between them in jeopardy. But did he do the right thing? What if this really was the end? What if he never had another opportunity?

"Yes, of course I do," he said.

"Then why didn't we? Why do we never do the things that we really want to do? Why do we always wait too long, until there isn't any time left? Tell me, James, why didn't we?"

"I don't know, Elena. Maybe because we can't live life like we're going to die tomorrow. Because I didn't know if our feelings were real. Because it has to mean more than just the physical act of sex. Because it would've been wrong. I don't know, maybe it's just that I always wait until it's too late."

"Yeah, well, fuck that."

"Yeah ... fuck that." James wrapped her up in his arms. "When this is all finished, maybe we can start over again."

Elena rested her head on his shoulder. "None of us can ever start over, James. But I just wish I could get him out of my mind. That it isn't his face I see when I go to sleep, that he doesn't still haunt my mind long after the night has passed. I wish my last memory of 'it' wasn't of him inside me. That my last memory of sex, of something that should be good and beautiful, wasn't with *him*. Who cares if it's right or wrong? I wish it could've been with you."

"I know. So do I." James gently freed himself from her arms, and they slowly started walking up the path, Elena still leaning on his shoulder with her arm around his back.

The house was clearly visible in the moonlight as James and Elena stood just within the edge of the forest near the south side of the house. It was a big beautiful old house commanding the hill with a vast sloping lawn in front of it, and trees rising with the mountain behind it. The mountains across the bay in the distance were only a dark outline against the night sky. The house was two stories and showed some of its age in the wood siding, where the weathering was visible even in the moonlight.

"There it is," Elena said. "The dark house in a forest in the middle of nowhere. Come on, let's circle around to the back."

They left the path and crept between the trees, heading toward the east side of the house where the forest edged closer to the back door, wincing each time one of them stepped on a twig or rustled some falling leaves. They stopped once more at the edge of the tree line, with the door they were headed for straight out in front of them.

"Are you ready for this?" James asked. After a brief hesitation, Elena nodded her head. His heart was beating wildly in his chest, and he felt a strange mixture of fear and exhilaration. He held up three fingers, counted down to one, then burst out of the tree line in a full sprint.

He wasn't even halfway across the lawn when he felt a sharp sting in his right shoulder. James stopped, his mind frantically trying to figure out what had just happened. He looked over and saw the dart. He dropped to his knees, grabbed the dart with his left hand, and slowly pulled it out. Somehow they had failed, and he hadn't even gotten to the house yet. He looked around for Elena, but it was too dark to see anything. A heavy, watery sensation spread through his body as he fell onto his back.

James thought he could hear voices. He tried to open his eyes, but found it difficult. Blurry images started to appear as he tried to force himself out of the fog. Then he noticed the pain in his head, a pain that jolted through him with each heartbeat.

He looked around and could tell that he was in a large, open room. It was dark though, and he couldn't see much. He tried to reach up to feel what was causing the throbbing pain in his head, but something was restraining his arm. His legs as well. He realized that he was tied to a chair. He tried to remember where he was. Suddenly, his stomach convulsed, and he thought he was going to throw up.

He turned his head. There was a woman, also tied to a chair. Elena. Then he remembered.

"Ah, I see you finally decided to join us in the cognizant world. Welcome, welcome."

James looked to see where the voice was coming from. There was a man sitting opposite of him, his face shrouded in shadow.

"Welcome to my humble abode. It seems you found the place all right. I wasn't sure exactly when to expect you, but you've arrived more or less on time. Sorry for the accommodations. I would've liked to treat you like proper guests, but then again, you didn't approach me as such, now did you? So now we have to meet like this. Unfortunate I know, but necessity is necessity."

The man got up from his seat and walked into the dim light cast by a lamp. He had longer black hair that was slicked back and a trimmed mustache and goatee. He was actually quite handsome, but there was a wild, unsettling look in his eyes. "The name's Cole, Cole Bontone."

James didn't reply. He looked over at Elena. She was awake, her head was down. Her expression was sad and empty.

"Don't worry, you don't need to introduce yourself. I already know your name, James Torbour. And Elena, well, she doesn't need any introduction, does she? I bet you're wondering what exactly happened, aren't you? Well, it's quite simple. You could have walked up to my front door and knocked like polite guests without ill intent, and you two would be dining on king salmon and drinking the finest of champagnes. Instead, you took it upon yourselves to skulk about like two thieves in the night. What you failed to realize is that you had tripped a motion detector hooked up to cameras when you walked past my DO NOT ENTER signs. And then, I also had to calibrate the correct dosage of tranquilizer for each of you so that it wouldn't kill you or anything, and although you were out for a little longer than expected, it seems to have worked out quite well. Elena here has been up for almost an hour, but hasn't said a word this whole time. Terrible company. It's a shame, we used to have such good times together."

"You have a strange idea of good times then, you psychopathic rapist fuck," James said, surprised by his own boldness.

In an instant, Cole lashed out, kicking James's chair backward. His head bounced in a flare of agonizing pain as the chair slammed onto the floor. Everything was still spinning when a fist came crashing into his face.

"Show some respect, fucker!" Cole yelled, leaning over James. "You are in my house now, and you will show some respect to your host."

"Or what, you'll kill me?" James spat some blood off to the side. "What are you waiting for then?"

Cole's face softened, and he pulled James's chair upright. Chuckling to himself, he said, "Kill you? No, I'm not going to kill you. I'm not going to kill anyone if I don't have to." He brushed James's hair back into place, then took out a handkerchief and wiped the blood off his face. "Don't be so melodramatic, James. I didn't go through all this work just to kill you. That would be such a waste. You'll see, all in good time. The night is still young, and there's no reason to rush so hastily toward the end."

Cole took a step back as if he was thinking of what to do next. After a moment's pause, he stepped toward Elena. "Let's not forget about Elena, dear sweet ... or perhaps not so sweet Elena. Oh, I had such high hopes for you, but you turned out to be just another ingrate, didn't you?"

Elena continued to stare at the ground with the same blank look of sadness since James had come to.

"Look at me when I'm talking to you, Elena. LOOK AT ME!" Elena snapped her head up, now with fear on her face. "That's better. It didn't have to come to this, you know. We could have made it work between us. I know that there's a part of you that still loves me. You had to throw it all away, though, and for what? You devise this little scheme of yours and think you can live happily ever after? You must have known it could never work. You're not that naïve, and I'm not that stupid."

"I never loved you," Elena said in a voice that was shocking in its clarity and sternness. "The last few days that

I have spent with James were worthy of being the last days of my life. And anything is better than giving you the satisfaction of having me for even one more day."

"You see that?" Cole asked, smiling at James. "A fire stills burns in that one. I think that's what attracted me to her in the first place. Where I found her, she was just a junkie and a whore, but she had that fire. No doubt you know what I mean." He fell silent again for a moment. "Well, you know what? I think we'll have that dinner after all."

Only a half hour later, the table was set, and the meal was ready. Cole dragged James and then Elena to the table, still tied to their chairs. They sat across from each other at one end of the large rectangular table. After freeing their arms, Cole took his seat at the head of the other side. A semi-automatic shotgun rested on the table beside his plate. In front of each person was an artful arrangement of a fillet of salmon, whipped potatoes, and a tangle of greens twisted into a delicate cone.

Some kind of last meal, James thought. *Like I'm on death row or something. No, that's exactly what this is. Despite whatever he may have said, he has no intentions of just letting us go.*

"Now even though you two came here with ill intent," Cole said, "let's let bygones be bygones. I can't really blame you, anyway. I even expected it. You had to do what you thought was right. Oh!" He smacked his forehead. "But we're missing one thing."

Cole hurried out of the room and came back momentarily with a bottle in his hand. "This is one of the finest champagnes in the world, and it's not cheap. This is a bottle of Krug Clos Du Mesnil. It is a Chardonnay created from grapes harvested from a single vineyard. I don't indulge in this kind of luxury often, but this occasion is special enough to deserve such decadence, don't you think?"

James just poked at the outer layers of the salmon with his fork, like a child who doesn't like his food and has no intention of eating it. His mind drifted to other things, to how he would—

A knife came crashing down onto James's plate, splitting the fillet in half and making James jump against his restraints.

"You just have to get in there and start eating it," Cole said, his voice loud but somehow jovial. "Don't play with your food, just eat. That's fresh king salmon. I wish I could take responsibility for catching it, but I don't find myself on the open waters as much as I would like." He poured a glass of champagne for James and then walked over to Elena. "Don't be so sad, my dear. Enjoy the food." He filled her glass while looking at the untouched plate in front of her. "Or if you're not going to eat, at least try the champagne. Trust me, it's the best thing you'll ever drink."

Then Cole made his way to his own chair again and started digging into his food.

James chewed a little chunk of salmon, then forced himself to swallow. It tasted like nothing, and lodged in his chest. He sipped his champagne, wincing as the carbonation burned his mouth and nose. *How do we get out of this? He has that shotgun. Maybe I should have stabbed him with my fork when he was pouring the champagne. Maybe I can do it if he comes by again.* He took another drink, wincing again. *But what good would that do? I don't have anything to follow it up with. Maybe I can untie these ropes without him noticing. I have to do something. I have to try and save her ... somehow ... whatever the cost.*

"You know, it's too quiet," Cole said. "Come on, let's have some conversation. I know you must have questions, so go ahead, ask me anything. I'll answer anything I'm able to."

"Well, now that you mention it, there is one thing I am rather curious about," James said, figuring that things could hardly get worse. "Something happened to George and Anna Green, and something tells me that you might know what."

Cole gave him a slight smile, and then took a drink of his champagne, emptying his glass. "Yes, no doubt you would be curious about them—it's their house you've been living at, after all. Well, as it happens I do know exactly what happened to them. It was about a month ago, maybe a little longer. I had met Anna only twice before, and only just in passing ..."

Chapter 16

GEORGE AND ANNA: ONE MONTH EARLIER

Cole walked into the living room of his home and stopped abruptly. Sitting on his favorite chair was a woman looking right back at him with an icy stare. "Well, well, well, isn't this a pleasant surprise?" he said. "It's always a true pleasure to see you."

Anna raised the shotgun that she had been holding at the side of the chair and pointed it at him. It was a single-barreled break action shotgun, so it only held one shell chambered, but one shot was all she needed.

Cole gave her a slight and rather off smile. He had a look in his eyes, but it wasn't one of fear. "So it's like that then, is it?" He pulled a chair from the side of the room and sat directly opposite of her.

"I see you, I see what you are," Anna said.

"So you do. And this is your plan, then? To shoot me, to murder an unarmed man in cold blood? A man who has never done you ill."

"You may not have done me any physical harm, but I know what you've done. You've gone unchecked for too long, doing that which thou wilt. Well no more, your reckoning has come."

"And who are you to be judge, jury, and executioner?" Cole asked. "You may think you know me, but do you really? Can you trust your dreams, these feelings that you base your whole reality upon? What if you are simply crazy, and it's all in your head? I'm sure you've questioned it yourself."

Cole watched her face change—just slightly, but the change was there—and how she shifted in her chair. "Yes, George has told me all about it," he continued. "We've become quite good friends. So what's your plan here? After you kill me, what will you do? How will ol' Georgie react to what you've done? Do you think he would possibly forgive you?"

Cole paused again to gauge the response on Anna's face. "You don't, do you? No, you know you can't move on from this. You don't want to either, do you? So this is your way out then, the end of the road for both of us. Do you really believe you can leave this world in peace by killing me, though? As if by killing me you've served your purpose in life and can finally earn the death that you desire? Of course, yours isn't the only life you will take with you—George will inevitably follow you into that eternal darkness before long."

"Shut up!" Anna yelled. "You have no right to talk about George!"

"He may think you're batshit crazy, yet somehow he still seems to hopelessly love you. Don't ask me why after everything it seems like you've put him through. I don't think he could take it, not after everything else. I can see you know I'm right."

The shotgun started to tremble. Anna's face, which had been so stern and resolute, was now broken as she looked at him mutely, almost beseeching him.

Cole looked at his watch. "Look, if the two of you want to kill each other, go ahead. What the fuck do I care? If you want to blow me away, pull the trigger. But do you mind allowing me one small indulgence before you do?" Cole slowly pulled a cigar case from his pocket and took out a cigar.

He lit his cigar and they sat in silence, Cole smoking his cigar and Anna trying to hold the shotgun steady.

There was a sudden sound of a door opening, then slamming shut. George entered the room with a handgun gripped in both hands.

"Anna? Thank God you're okay. What's going on here?"

"Oh us, we're just having a little chat," Cole said. "It's nice of you to join us."

"What are you doing here?" Anna asked. "No, this is all wrong. How did you find me?"

"George has been here before," Cole said. "He just hasn't told you. But I guess he doesn't tell you a great many things these days, doesn't he?"

"She was right, wasn't she?" George asked Cole, turning his gun on him. "She was right about you all along?"

"You should be more willing to accept things that you cannot see with your eyes. There are a great many things that exist beyond the physical realm of this world. If you understood that, then maybe we wouldn't be in this pickle."

"George, you shouldn't be here. This doesn't involve you," Anna said as she got up from the chair and stepped forward.

"The hell it doesn't involve me! Anna, I know what you are about to do. I know you believe that this is the only way, but it's not. I know I haven't been there for you over the past few months, but things can still be different. I believe you, Ann. I'm sorry I never did before, but I truly do now. We can still walk away from this. It's not too late."

As George and Anna stared at each other, their weapons limply pointed toward Cole, Cole reached behind his jacket and, in one smooth motion, pulled two gleaming chrome pistols from the back of his waistband, one in each hand. Before either George or Anna could react, he had the gun in his left hand trained on George and the one in his right hand on Anna.

"Now, now, let's not rush toward any quick reactions here," Cole said. "Or none of us might walk out of here alive. George is right, you can still walk away from here. That is, if you can bear the thought of leaving me up here, alive and free to do that which I will." A subtle smile came across Cole's face as he finished speaking.

A moment of silence followed, with the three of them pointing their respective weapons at each other.

"I came here to kill him," Anna said. "He's evil, George! He's lived up here too long, free and unchecked. I'm here to put an end to it."

"I realize now that he's evil, but you don't need to kill him," George said. "That's not your responsibility. Anna, you don't need to kill yourself either, that's not the only way out."

Anna looked at George, tears beginning to spill from her eyes. "Just walk away? Leave him? How could I find peace like that? Knowing that he's still up here, that the dreams will never stop, that I will never find rest, never find peace? I must kill him, I must do something that has true meaning, something with a real purpose. Then I can find my own rest, I can find a place for myself to lie down and sleep. There is no peace for me in life, if only you could see that this *is* the only way for me."

"But it isn't, Anna. It can't be. You know that I love—"

"Why are you here?! You're not supposed to be here! This is my fate, not yours."

"And what about me? What's my fate? Don't you love me any more?"

Anna just looked at him, tears still streaming from her eyes.

Cole aimed both guns at George and emptied two rounds into the center of his chest. Multiple gunshots rang out, concussing the air. George had managed to fire his weapon, but his shot went astray. Anna had fired her shotgun at Cole, center mass, and watched him fall to the ground. Anna dropped the gun and rushed to where George was lying on the floor. There was already a large amount of blood pooling on the floor around him.

"George, George, I'm sorry, I'm so sorry. This is my fault, this is all my fault. George, I love you, of course I still love you. You know that, don't you? I've always loved you."

Looking back up at her, George was able to very faintly say, "I know." Then, after a moment, his eyes went vacant.

As Anna was kneeling at his side, something came crashing down onto her right shoulder and the back of her head. She fell down onto the floor along with a few fragments of wood. Sharp shoots of pain traced the nerves throughout her upper body as she turned onto her elbow. She saw a shadowy shape hover above her, and as her vision cleared, she saw that it was Cole.

Cole tossed what was left of the frame of a chair off to the side. "Fucking bitch," he said, and kicked away the handgun that was lying next to George. Then he unzipped his jacket to reveal a Kevlar vest.

Anna could see the scattered buckshot from her shotgun imprinted on it. His shoulder was bleeding; the vest hadn't taken all of the impact. Anna started to get up, but before she could, Cole yanked her up by her hair and shoved her against the wall. She let out a stifled scream as Cole pressed a gun to her forehead with such force that blood started to trickle down. Hatred filled his face as he looked at her.

"Do it. Go on, pull the trigger," Anna said. "Don't be a pussy now, I know you want to. This is what you were waiting for, isn't it?"

Cole's face softened, and he pulled the gun slightly away from her forehead. "No, that's what *you* want. That's what you've always wanted, isn't it? As much as you wanted to kill me, you wanted to die even more. Well, I'm not going to give you the satisfaction. No, you'll have to live with what you've done. Because you caused this, this is your fault, not mine. I'm not the one that came up here looking to kill you."

Cole let go of her, and Anna collapsed to the floor. He was correct in one thing at least, she thought as she wept— she did want to die, more now than ever. But she still wanted to do one last thing first. She thought that she had been shown Cole's true self so that she could put an end to him. That she could still do something good and meaningful before the end. But somehow, none of it had worked out like she thought it would. And now what was she left with?

"Yes, you will go out, back into the world," Cole said, "scraping and clawing for some kind of meaning or purpose. Ever looking for some semblance of your former life, wondering how you could've ever been so discontent with everything you once had. Looking for happiness and peace, but never being able to find it. Until one day, long after all hope is long gone, you finally lie down to die, cold and alone, with nothing left but the darkness to take you in. That is the fate that awaits you, Anna. That is the fate that you deserve."

As Anna lay on the floor crying, her eyes locked on the broken chair leg that Cole had smashed over her. It was jagged at the end where it had broken off. After taking one last look at George, she slowly reached for the chair leg. As she got to her feet, she swung around, and with a wide sweeping motion she aimed for his neck. Cole saw what she was doing at the last instant and tried to duck out of the way. It was enough to make her miss his neck, but the splintered wood sank deeply into his injured shoulder. Cole screamed in pain and stumbled away from her. Anna stood there looking at him, not knowing what to do.

Cole grabbed hold of the chair leg and slowly pulled it from his shoulder. He screamed in agony as it slowly made its way through his flesh. Then he glared at Anna, holding the chair leg in his hand as his blood dripped off it and onto the floor.

Horror distorted Anna's face and she turned, about to run. Then she saw George's gun lying on the floor and made a dash for it.

Cole was right behind her, and as she scrambled for the gun, he made a downward strike with the broken chair leg, scoring a long gash down her back. She fell to the floor and crawled for the gun. Just as her fingers touched it, a boot came crushing down onto her hand and she howled in pain. The second boot kicked the gun away. She rolled over and looked up at him.

Blood was steadily coming down his shoulder, but he seemed to give it no heed. He had a slight smile, and his eyes shined wildly as he looked down at her. With his free hand, he reached down and grabbed hold of her hair at the roots, and pulled her up to her feet and against the wall. She let out a quick yelp as she was being pulled up, and then she fell silent again.

With his right hand, Cole stabbed the splintered chair leg into Anna's stomach with one forceful and deliberate strike. He watched as she gasped at the impact, noted the pain on her face. Then, with the same forceful strength and deliberation, he stabbed her an additional five times in her midsection in quick succession. The splintered point on the chair leg broke off on the last stab, embedded in her stomach, and Cole tossed what was left of it off to the side. Blood was coming out of her mouth, and he still held her there until he finally saw the life leave her eyes. Then he finally let go of her hair and let her body fall limply to the floor. He looked at her lying there like that for a few moments. Then he walked outside and lit a cigar.

Chapter 17

JAMES AND ELENA: DAY 6, PART 3

Cole looked back and forth between James and Elena, at their solemn faces. "One can never truly know how things will end up, how things will all unfold," he said as he rubbed his shoulder, where his wound still hadn't completely healed. "Anna came to me looking for death, and that is what she found. I never touched a hair on her head before then. I never did a thing to either of them, yet she came to me unprovoked with the intention of killing *me*. Was I not justified in defending myself? Am I the bad guy because I did what was necessary for my own self-preservation? As for George, he made his choice as well. Sometimes things just happen. Shortly after that I met Elena, and I'm sure she has probably filled you in on all of that, at least her version of it, anyway." After a momentary pause, he added, "More champagne, anyone?"

For the rest of the meal, no one said a word.

"Well, let's take this outside, shall we? It's a beautiful night, and a full moon. Well, the full moon is actually tomorrow night, but close enough, right?"

Cole grabbed the semi-automatic shotgun from the table and slung it over his shoulder. He pulled out a knife and then a handgun from his holster, and pointing the gun at the back of James's head, he cut the ropes that were binding him to his chair. "No funny business now, okay?" Then Cole slowly made his way around to Elena while keeping his gun aimed at James, and did the same with her. When they were in front of him, he sheathed his knife and then unslung the shotgun from his shoulder, tucked the handgun back into its holster, and aimed the shotgun at them. "I don't want to use this, so don't make me, okay? Put your hands on your heads, and we're going to make our way outside."

James and Elena filed out the door with their hands on their heads, followed by Cole with his shotgun ever trained at their backs. James looked over at Elena, who glanced at him for only an instant before returning her gaze to the ground.

"My, my, isn't it just beautiful out here?" Cole said. He stared up at the cloudless sky for a moment, then pulled a zippo out of his pocket, sparked the flint wheel, and dropped it to the ground. Immediately, a trail of fire shot out along the grass, lighting several larger fires as it went along. When the fire stopped making its path, there were three larger fires on either side of an open area of grass leading toward an overlook of the bay down below. At the end of these fires was one slightly larger fire situated between the two fires farthest from them, set right before a steep drop, almost like a cliff. The line of fire that lit the larger fires burned out, leaving the seven fires to form a large open-ended rectangle with only three sides.

"Please, please, put your hands down. You look like a pair of idiots standing there like that. There's no need for that now," Cole said, lowering his gun slightly but still keeping it at the ready. "Now I know you're probably wondering what you're doing out here, and maybe you think I'm just going to kill you. But as I said before, I don't want to do that. You know, I can't help thinking of all the years I've spent in this house, all the history. I think about whether it was all worth it, the things I've done, the life I've lived. Years ago, I built up a reputation for this house, a place for people to come to and escape from the dullness of their lives. A house of pleasure, and of mysteries. Eventually, I started to get bored with that life, of being a host to these sick, annoying, and disgusting people. So I stopped entertaining people altogether and spent the next couple of years more or less alone.

"Naturally, though, as time went on, I got lonely and bored being by myself for so much time. The thing I had found most fascinating when I was still entertaining people here was their behavior. What they would do, how they would act or react to their situation. I had started to invite a few women here again, but I found it all rather dull. Yet human behavior still fascinated me, and I had a desire, a need, to take things further. So after much careful planning, I took a woman here that was, how should I put it ... less than willing. The high, the exhilaration I felt when I took her here, it was like nothing else. To see something that you like and just take it, it's such a freeing and powerful experience. She enthralled me. She was the first, and I spent a great deal of time with her. I was very kind and hospitable to her for the most part, and she always seemed to keep my interest, whether by her varying moods, or her changing tactics in trying to get me to let her go. This new experiment into human behavior pleased me very much, and I felt encouraged to continue with it. I took another woman here, and eventually another one after that. I loved seeing how they would act so similarly in certain ways, and quite differently in other ways, each of them unique and fascinating. It was constantly a fresh experience, and I learned a great deal about human behavior and emotion.

"Eventually, I stopped doing that as well. Not so much out of guilt—I was much beyond that by now—or because I feared being caught, but because I craved new experiences. It was also the time when I first met George and Anna. Now I knew Anna was quite unique, and different than anyone else I had ever met before. She immediately saw straight through into who I really was. No one had ever done that before, and I had to know more about her. So I befriended George and learned all I could about her. I had come to know long ago that there are forces at work beyond that which we can see with the physical eye, things that we cannot fully see or comprehend. I have seen some strange things in my life, and it seemed quite clear to me that there were elements at play beyond our physical grasp. As things progressed, I saw the opportunity for another type of experiment in human behavior, if you will. When Anna came up to my house, she triggered the same alarm that you did, and so I made my way down to let George know where she would be. I was able to lead them both into a moment of confrontation with each other and me, and it was exhilarating to see what would happen."

Cole took out a cigar from his pocket and lit it. After he took a few puffs he continued. "I'm sorry, I can get a little carried away sometimes talking about the past. I guess it's because I don't talk to people very often any more. After what happened with George and Anna, I found Elena, and she also seemed different than anyone I had met before in her own way. Unlike most people in her situation, she had this … quality, this essence about her. Sure, it was buried beneath the drugs and dirt and self-hate, but I could still see it. There was something there, and it intrigued me. An idea struck me then, 'Who is this person?' If I could take her out of this filth that she was living in, if I could get her off the drugs, what kind of person would she be? I was very curious about her, so I brought her back here and helped her get better. I loved her, in my own way, but I know I'm not an easy man to love in return, and I don't blame Elena for what she did. Elena, well, she is a good person, and I am not. It became clear to me that nothing would work out between us, but I didn't want all the time I had invested in her to go to waste.

"James, I was aware of your presence at the house along the shore. So I looked into who you were and your background. I decided that I had the opportunity to turn this into yet another experiment of sorts. So I made my deal with Elena." Cole paused, staring at the sky once again, and then looked right at Elena. "What I never told you, Elena, was that I never expected you to do as I said. I knew you weren't the kind of person who would follow through on something like that. No, my plan all along was to see what two people such as yourselves would do in the situation that I placed you in. I wanted to see if you would tell James the truth, or withhold it from him, if you would turn against each other or fall in love. And most of all, what you would end up doing when ..." Cole trailed off as he dropped the butt of his cigar and ground the heel of his boot into it.

Cole ambled over to Elena and stood a few feet in front of her. "Elena, Elena, Elena ... hmm, you didn't quite hold up your end of the bargain, did you? And yet both of you are here, you both came to me voluntarily. Yes, perhaps it was for ill intent, but still, here you are." Tilting her head up with his hand so that she was looking at him, he quietly said, "I will still honor my end of our bargain. You brought James up here, therefore you are free to leave ... if that is what you still wish for."

A look of confusion, fear, and hope came across her face, but mostly there was fear. She looked over at James questioningly, still not completely sure what Cole's intentions were. James looked back at her with a blank face that she couldn't read.

"Or ..." Cole said, much louder now as he walked over toward James. "Or perhaps *you* can walk away from here, free and unscathed, free to do what you will." Cole looked up toward the night sky and breathed in deeply. "It's beautiful, isn't it?" Then he looked from James to Elena. "One of you can walk away from here, one of you can't. Blood has to be spilled tonight, that's just the way it is, there isn't any way around that, but only one of you has to die. On that rock over there, down on the end where that big fire is burning, there is a knife. Oh, and if you can't decide who will die or simply choose not to play along, you both will die. And I can guarantee you that it will be a much more unpleasant way to go. One of you must kill yourself so that the other can live. I give you my solemn word that the one who lives can walk away from here free and unscathed. And above all, I am a man of my word."

James and Elena looked at each other. Elena's face was full of sorrow. James's face was a mixture of fear and conflict.

"Now is the time. Choose," Cole said as he backed away and disappeared into shadow.

James looked at Elena again. She was looking right into his eyes, but still she didn't say a word. There was so much emotion in that silent face. It was partly apologetic, partly sad, and partly hopeless. But in that face, he also saw love, and it was perhaps the only time that James truly knew for sure that she really did love him. If there had been a window of opportunity for escape, a way to get them both out of this alive, he had missed it. No, there was no more time to make a play, to escape this final darkness. But perhaps it wasn't too late to do something. To perform one final act that had true meaning and purpose. A way to perhaps somehow make it all worth it in the end, knowing that it hadn't all been meaningless. He didn't want to die, not now, but that didn't matter any more. He felt a kind of peace settle in on him as he started to fully realize his fate.

James went up to Elena and kissed her passionately. Pulling away slightly, he said, "I love you, Elena. You can still find a life out there for yourself. You are strong, and you will get past this. You will live a full and happy life. You have to." He kissed her again. "I'm sorry I failed you."

Still looking back at her as he walked away, he pulled his hand from the iron grip she had on it. Tears were coming down his face now, and still Elena was unable to speak. As James kept walking away from her and closer to that knife glinting with reflected fire in the distance, she couldn't stay quiet any longer.

"NOOOO!" Elena screamed. "NO! You can't! James, you can't do this!" She ran after him and in an adrenalized frenzy, grabbed him by his shoulders and threw him down onto his back. She ran to the rock, then she slowly picked up the knife, staring at the blade.

"Elena!" James yelled as he got back up. "What are you doing? Come back, don't do this, Elena!" He ran after her, but as she turned around to face him with the knife gripped in one hand, he stopped in place with only about ten yards separating them. "Elena, don't do this! It's supposed to be me—it should be me! Please don't do this, Elena!"

"No James, it's supposed to be me. I brought all of this on, this is my fault. This is what I deserve, I'm not a good person. This is where my story ends, but yours doesn't have to. It can't. What we had together was a dream, a dream and nothing more. This can still mean something, though. Yes, I can see it. This is how it has to be. This is right. It's up to you, James, to do the right thing. Move on, but don't forget about me."

Time seemed to slow down, Elena looked at peace, and even with the slight shakiness in her hand, she seemed calm as she brought the knife up to her throat. She looked James in the eyes again. "Don't forget about me, James." Then she slid the knife across her throat in one clean and smooth motion. Blood poured out from her neck, a red stain spreading down her coat.

"NO, ELENA, NOOOO!" James screamed as he ran toward her. He caught her body just as she fell. She looked into his eyes and started to raise her hand up to his face, and then dropped it back down. As James knelt with Elena in his arms, he looked down at her and saw the life pass from her eyes. "NOOOO!" James screamed into the sky. "Elena ... why ... why did you do this?! Why did you have to do this?" Tears fell from his face and onto Elena's. "You can't leave me yet. Oh God, what have you done? It was supposed to be me, it should've been me. Why did you do it? What am I supposed to do now?"

James fell silent, and silence surrounded him. No sounds of crickets, no hooting of owls, only silence as he held Elena's limp body and stared into her lifeless eyes. Some unknowable time later, a voice brought him back out of the void.

"It looks different than you thought it would, doesn't it?"

James spun around and saw Cole standing a few yards away from him, shotgun still in his hand. "The way things end up. You picture things happening a certain way, you continue to hope beyond all hope until the very end. You believe that things might still work out, that despite everything that tells you differently, you still believe that you can climb out of the darkness, and that perhaps the two of you could walk off into the sunset in the end." Cole shrugged. "But here you are, staring at the one you lost, the one you loved."

James was about to yell back at him. Scream all kinds of obscenities at the sick son of a bitch that took her away from him. But then he felt that there wasn't any point, and his grief was still too strong. So he just looked back down at Elena and said nothing.

Cole turned to walk away, motioning with his shotgun for James to follow him. Not knowing what else to do, James gently laid Elena's body down onto the grass off to the side of the pool of blood that had formed below her and followed him. Cole took a seat on a rock in front of one of the fires that was still burning. Reaching into his shirt pocket, he pulled out his cigar case. He took two cigars out, offering one to James, but James just stood there with his arms at his sides. Cole shrugged, replaced one of the cigars, and then lit the other one.

"Why are we here?" he asked, expelling a cloud of smoke. "What are we doing? What are we going to do?

These are the questions we all ask ourselves, the questions you have no doubt asked yourself many times. I honestly didn't know how it would all turn out, you know. I didn't know what I expected I would feel, some kind of satisfaction I suppose. But I don't feel anything, just emptiness. I'm getting old, not really old, but old. I can feel it. But tell me, James, what have I really taken from you? Tell me, what would you have done if I hadn't done what I did?" His voice was getting louder now. "Would you two spend the rest of your lives together? What then? Would you not hate each other in the end, would you not despise each other? Better that it ends now rather than later. Better that you don't have to grow old together, and at the end of life have nothing other than hate for each other, nothing more than sorrow and despair at the end of your days."

The end of his cigar glowed red in the dark as Cole inhaled. "Do you know what it's like to see something that you want and just take it? No, of course you don't. If you did you would've taken Elena before it was too late. Yes, I know all about that. Don't you think that I would keep a sharp eye on you two? And I gotta say I don't get it, when you want her and she wants you, that you still do nothing. I know you hate me, I know you want to kill me, and I don't blame you. It's curious the way things end up. For instance, I didn't quite expect that you would both be so willing to sacrifice yourselves for each other. I'll come right out and say it, James, I'm almost a little envious. Despite the life of luxury and pleasure that I've lived, I have never felt a love that would make me want to die for another person. Anyhow, you are free to leave as I said you would be, if that's what you still wish. If it isn't ... well, why are we here? What are we doing? What have we done? What are we going to do?" He grabbed a gun from the back of his waistband. The same Sig Sauer that James had brought with him. "There's only one bullet, use it wisely." Cole tossed the gun onto the grass, and then started to back away into the shadow.

"Wait!" James yelled out, his voice strained and heavy with grief. "But why? Why do this? What were you trying to prove?"

Cole paused at the edge of the shadow. "James, haven't you been listening?" he said in a kind and almost sympathetic voice. "I wasn't trying to prove anything. I was just curious to see what would happen. But I'm not some kind of monster as you probably think I am. I don't find joy in your suffering. And although you probably find it hard to believe, I am also sad to see Elena dead. Do what thou wilt, James." Cole turned and disappeared into the shadow. "Death comes to us all."

James walked to the gun and picked it up. He felt a powerful urge to run into the darkness and search for Cole, to drive that one bullet into his head, to have his revenge. But as he dropped out the magazine to confirm that in fact there was one and only one bullet in the magazine and then that the chamber was empty, he thought, *What is the point?* Did he really want to go out into that black forest with nothing but one bullet? He looked at the blood on his chest and arms, her blood. He looked back over at her body. He couldn't stand leaving Elena there, all on her own, all by herself. So instead of going out into the dark to try to satisfy his hate and to have his revenge, he walked back to where the body of Elena lay, not yet able to let her go.

He fell down onto his knees beside her, fresh tears falling down his face again. She still had a look of sadness on her pale face. As he looked at her, he remembered his dream from the night before. It was different than all the dreams he could ever remember having, more vivid with a sense of urgency and importance. At the time, he had shrugged it off as nothing more than just a dream, and it quickly faded away as the burdens of the coming day weighed down upon him. But for some reason, it came back to him now, and he remembered it just as vividly as he had when he first awakened from it.

James stood at the edge of the shore, the waves washing past the heels of his shoes. He stared at the horizon, where the sky and the water melted into one. He was wondering what lay beyond the horizon. He realized that he was in a moment so timeless and beautiful that he felt he would never forget this moment and all that it held. His mind was free and relaxed. If he could just hang on to this feeling, if he could just stay in this state of mind, where everything was wonderful and beautiful.

He could hear music. He couldn't place the exact words, or the band that was playing, but it was the most beautiful and heartfelt music he had ever heard. He closed his eyes and let the music and the feeling take him away. When he opened his eyes again, there was nothing but water surrounding him. It was dark out, yet somehow he could see far out beyond him. The music was gone and all was silent. Suddenly, he saw something out of the corner of his eye. At first he thought it was just a log, then he saw that it was a body. It was a woman, she was floating face down and he couldn't see her face. When he first dreamed it he had no idea who it could be, although looking back at it now he could swear that she looked eerily similar to Elena with her blonde hair.

As he was staring at the body floating by him, it started to turn over. But just as her face turned up and James thought he would be able to see who it was, her hair shrouded her face. Then she sank into the water and disappeared. The water, which James stared into as if waiting for her to reappear, grew darker and darker until there was nothing but blackness.

Sometime later, James found himself climbing up a mountain. He had the feeling that he was seeking refuge from some impending doom. Built into the rock of a sheer cliff, he saw a door leading into the body of the mountain. He turned the handle and walked through. Inside was a large room, all white with a glossy finish and many more doors on the walls. It seemed very strange, sterile. Suddenly, the room became very crowded with people. They were all frightened and scared, although of what, James had no idea. The ground started to shake, clouds of dust and dirt started falling from the ceiling. The walls started closing in, the whole room seemed to be collapsing upon itself in some unreal and abstract way. James quickly turned around and left through the door that he had come in through.

He was back outside on the mountain. Out in the distance, he saw a massive fireball that was developing into an enormous mushroom cloud. He spun and ripped open the same door, desperate to escape the devastation outside. Again, he found himself in a white room. Only this time, it was different. There were no walls, only the white floor he stood on, which expanded in all directions until it melded with the white light that surrounded him. The surrounding space was completely empty. Then he noticed there was a table, also white, and on that table was a phone, a phone that was completely black, the only thing in the room that wasn't white. It was an old-fashioned phone, one with the rotary dial with the numbers on the face of it. James slowly walked toward the table, and as he got close to it, the phone started to ring. After the fifth ring, and with some hesitation, James finally picked it up.

"Hello, James," came a deep yet peaceful voice from the other end. "I have been watching you. I have given you so much time, and so many chances, yet what have you done with them? Now it's almost time, you can still do the right thing—"

James slammed the phone down, afraid of what the voice might say. A moment later, the phone rang again. Fear petrified him, but the phone kept ringing, and he reluctantly picked up the receiver, holding it to his ear.

"You know what you have to do," said a voice, this one different than the last, somehow both ominous and soothing at the same time. "There is no reason to fear. A beautiful peace awaits you, where there is no loneliness, no despair, no agony. You know what you have to do."

James set the phone down once again, and a bright light blinded him. When he managed to open his eyes again, he stood on a dirt path in a thick forest. The space surrounding him seemed to fluctuate; the trees seeming to close in and then pull back away. There was a dark figure on the path in front of him, completely cloaked in black, with a hood concealing its face. It held out a gloved hand and pointed down the path, where it blended into the darkness. Then the dark figure disappeared. James hesitated, then started to walk down the path toward where it was pointing. The trees around him started to dissolve and then disappeared completely. He was on a green grassy plain that seemed to go on forever. Out in front of him there was something that resembled a sunset, yet was somehow different, otherworldly. A crystalline light spread out into many different colors as it melded with the blue sky above. As he stared at this magnificent horizon, the ground suddenly gave way in front of him, and the light in the distance faded and revealed a night sky filled with stars. He seemed to be back in the world he knew once again. He was standing on the edge of a cliff, and all he could see was darkness beneath him. Then he leaned forward and felt himself falling through the blackness that surrounded him.

James felt like he still understood little of the dream's meaning, if, in fact, it had any. But he now thought that it accentuated the choice that now lay in front of him. He reached down and stroked Elena's bloody hand with his own. "I'm sorry I couldn't protect you. I failed you, you were drowning in the darkness and I couldn't save you. Be at peace, you are in the light now. The darkness can never touch you again." Then, after a moment of silence, he cried out, "Why didn't you let me do it? It should have been me! Why wasn't it me?"

James looked at the gun for a long moment. Then he racked the slide back and let it fly forward—the noise of it snapping back into place momentarily filling the space around him. He looked up at the sky, cloudless and full of so many stars. He looked across the bay and to the shadow of the mountains in the distance. It was all so beautiful. He then looked back down at Elena, also still beautiful, even in death. "This is good, isn't it?" His vision blurred with tears as he slowly put the barrel up underneath his chin. He looked down at Elena once more and then looked up into the sky. Slowly, and with his hands slightly shaking, he placed his finger over the trigger.

A voice came into his head—something that Elena had said to him. *What is there to live for? How about life itself? And that even if it's not so great, you still keep on living it, because that's what you do. You find some kind of reason, or a hope that things will get better someday. And even if they don't, maybe you get one moment, one moment that's so beautiful that it makes going through everything that's terrible in this life worth it.* Then he heard her say, *It's up to you, James, to do the right thing. Move on, but don't forget about me.*

James jerked the gun out from under his jaw, and the gun fell out of his hands. It hit a rock, bounced, and tumbled over the cliff. James fell to his knees and reached out to grab it, but it was already gone.

He slowly got up to his feet and then looked back down at Elena's body. Then he looked over toward the blackness of the forest. He bent down and pulled the knife from the tight grip that she still held it with. He looked at the blood-soaked blade, *her* blood, that still clung to its surface. He stood there for a while, looking at the blade and then at her body. The way he saw it, he had two options in front of him. He could try to avenge her. He could run after Cole into the forest, letting his hate and anger fuel him. But with what, a knife? Cole had a shotgun, and these were his woods. If James went after him, he faced almost certain death. But would that be so bad?

The other option was walking away. He knew that Cole would leave him alone if he left Cole alone as well. James could tell that he had a twisted sense of honor about these things, and that he would abide by his own rules. He looked back down at Elena. He couldn't just leave her here like this, with *him*. Who knew what he would do with her, what he would do to her.

Even if he somehow did manage to kill Cole, nothing would change. Elena would still be dead, and the pain he felt wouldn't go away. No, there was only one choice. He had a feeling, and somehow he was quite sure of it. He felt that maybe he didn't need to kill Cole anyway, that there was some greater force at work here that would see to Cole's rightful fate. *We all become what we deserve in the end.* With that thought, James tucked the knife through his belt at his side and bent down to pick up Elena's body. He hated how her dead weight felt in his arms. She was heavier than he thought she would be.

Beyond burying Elena, James had no idea what he was going to do. Perhaps hit the road and just drive until he found another place to stop. But where? He had nowhere to go. He was too full of grief and despair to think about any of that. He walked beyond the light of the dying fires and entered the darkness of the forest. As he disappeared into the night, he didn't have any hope of what the future might hold, or any belief that things would ever get better. But he was alive.

ACKNOWLEDGMENTS

I would like to thank my good friend Paul Keller for all of his encouragement and input from early on and throughout the entire process of writing this book. When I first showed him a very early draft of my story, he was very positive and was already urging me to eventually self-publish it, which I may never have done otherwise.

I would also like to thank my editor, Geoff Smith, for all the work he did in helping to form the book into the polished and cohesive work that it now is.

And also to my brother, Joe Neighbours, for his input and advice when I first showed it to him. As well as for all of his work that he did with making the cover art.

A special thanks to my parents, and everyone else who had an impact on this book in one way or another.

AUTHOR BIOGRAPHY

Up until I started writing this book, I never saw myself as a writer, or had much interest in it. I never thought I would be much good at it either. Then I started to get a desire to try my hand at writing something. So I sat down and soon after I started to write, the basic plot for The Darkness of Water came to me. I was very pleased and also surprised by how much I truly enjoyed writing this book. And as I continued to write, it eventually became what it now is.

I lived in Anchorage Alaska for two and a half years before moving back to my home state of Wisconsin. It was in Alaska where I wrote the vast majority of this book, which coincidentally is also the setting where the story takes place.

I love the idea of bringing stories to life that are sad, dark, and yet beautiful. There are many influences to my work. Such as David Lynch, a true master of film and surrealism, Alfred Hitchcock, Stephen King. And all the beautiful melancholic music like Daughter, Adna, and Many Rooms, that capture so well the mood that I tried to create in my own work.

www.ingramcontent.com/pod-product-compliance
Lightning Source LLC
Chambersburg PA
CBHW071906220626
47052CB00002B/227